STRONGER THAN THE SWORD

STRONGER
THAN THE
SWORD

Persecuted for righteousness' sake

Faith Cook

 BOOKS

EP Books
Faverdale North, Darlington, DL3 0PH, England
e-mail: sales@epbooks.org
web: www.epbooks.org

EP Books USA
P. O. Box 614, Carlisle, PA 17013, USA
e-mail: usasales@epbooks.org
web: www.epbooks.us

First published 2010

British Library Cataloguing in Publication Data available

ISBN-13 978 0 85234 728 7   ISBN 0 85234 728 6

Unless otherwise indicated, all Scripture quotations are from the
Authorized /King James Version

Scripture quotations marked 'ESV' are from The Holy Bible,
English Standard Version, published by HarperCollins Publish-
ers © 2001 by Crossway Bibles, a division of Good News Pub-
lishers. Used by permission. All rights reserved.

Printed and bound in Great Britain by JF Print Ltd, Sparkford,
Somerset

To my friend
Patricia Gibson — a great encourager

Contents

ILLUSTRATIONS

PREFACE AND ACKNOWLEDGEMENTS

As we listened to the news on one unforgettable evening in June 1978, we heard of an appalling massacre of Western missionaries at an Elim Pentecostal school in present-day Zimbabwe. Three men, six women and four children — one a baby of only three weeks old — had been bayoneted and mercilessly hacked to death. Mutilated almost beyond recognition, their bodies had been flung into the bush and abandoned. Slowly the names of the victims were read out one by one. We gasped with horror and dismay at the final name in the list: Wendy White, a close friend of ours. Later we heard that in those last harsh moments of life, Wendy had cried out to the others, 'Do not fear them that kill the body! They cannot kill the soul…' In that hour of extremity her faith had proved stronger than the cruel sword.

And so, down through the centuries, courageous Christians have embraced suffering and death rather than deny Jesus Christ. From Stephen, the first martyr of the early church, to our present day, countless numbers worldwide have demonstrated a faith in the living God stronger than the sword — a faith that prevails even though a civil power may attempt to crush and annihilate it.

Recollecting the sufferings of Wendy and her fellow missionaries in that remote African bush, together with those of an innumerable host who have 'loved not their lives even unto death', this story has been written. Based on a period in English church history between 1660 and 1688 known as 'The Great Persecution'— a time of relentless suffering for Dissenters — the narrative focuses on a typical family living in Somerset during these years. The circumstances of their lives are told in the context of the stirring historical events of the times and illustrate the surprising repercussions and rewards that may result from such spiritual faithfulness and sacrifice.

Of necessity the majority of the characters in *Stronger than the Sword* are fictitious, but they are representative of the true. Scattered throughout the story and interwoven with it, however, are references to a number of historical characters, men such as Joseph Alleine, John Bunyan, Hanserd Knollys, Lord Henry Wilmot, Judge George Jeffreys, Sir Matthew Hale and other political figures.

I am particularly grateful to four kind friends who have helped me with the illustrations for this book. Judy Holt has contributed some of her art work; Harold Gibson two of his paintings; while Chris and Alison Day have taken numerous photographs of Somerset scenery. Our friend Patricia Gibson has constantly encouraged me to persevere with the story, and my daughter Esther has read through my manuscript, making most helpful suggestions. As ever, I am indebted to Ralph Ireland, whose ability to spot mistakes in a text has saved many a writer from a host of verbal and grammatical errors. And mere words of thanks can never adequately express the debt I owe to the patience and encouragement of my husband, Paul.

It is my hope that this account, based on real-life events, may strengthen our own courage and determination to remain faithful to the truths of Scripture, cost what it may, and especially in these days when persecution is often presented in a host of subtle forms.

Faith Cook

1.

THE RESCUE

Nicholas Wilkes held his flickering lamp steadily in front
of him, its beam of light probing uncertainly through the
mists of that July night in 1645. Again and again he stumbled over the tufts of sedge grass that grew in clumps
everywhere across the moor. Mounds of peat loomed up
unexpectedly in the darkness. Here and there the stunted
trees cast weird shadows on the ground. Sometimes a
startled sheep bolted across his path and disappeared into
the night. Nicholas paid little notice. He was searching for
his son.

'James! James!' he called urgently, but nothing except
the eerie cry of night birds broke the silence. How different
it was from the clatter of horses' hooves, the yells of
cavalrymen and the roar of battle that had rampaged past
Moorside Farm that very afternoon! Sprawling on the edge
of bleak moorland, the farm, two miles from Langport in
Somerset, was known locally simply as Moorside, and was
currently owned by Nicholas Wilkes and his wife Alice.

A view of Langport today

Here the Wilkes family had bred Romney sheep — a rare long-haired breed — for many generations.

With the Civil War raging across the country since 1642, and the Royalists now facing defeat, Somerset men and women were deeply apprehensive. Everyone knew that the men of the Royalist army, led by the hard-drinking, unpredictable Lord George Goring, had been pillaging wherever they had been stationed. Hungry, angry and defeated yet again by Oliver Cromwell's well-trained troops at an engagement that became known as the Battle of Langport, they cared little whose property they robbed, or whose animals they killed, as they thundered past.

With the fighting so close, Nicholas had been concerned about the safety of his sheep grazing out on the moor not far from the farm and had sent his older son James to round up the flock and pen the animals securely in the field behind Moorside. But James had not returned. Many hours had passed since the disorderly troops had fled along the nearby path. Nicholas and Alice were growing ever more troubled about their son's safety. As darkness fell, the anxious father set out to look for James. This way and that he peered into the darkness. Then Nicholas heard a sound. A muffled moan seemed to come from low down in one of the treacherous ditches that criss-crossed the moor. Perhaps an animal had fallen down and was unable to find a way out, or perhaps…

Holding his lamp at arm's length, Nicholas scanned the length of the deep ditch as far as the beam would penetrate. Normally filled with water, the rhyne, as it was known locally, was dry; the unusually hot weather had left the soil cracked and hard. He could see nothing. Perhaps it had been his imagination. Calling his son's name repeatedly,

Nicholas stumbled on. Then he heard it again, only this time it sounded closer and more desperate. Somewhere nearby there must be an injured animal, or even a man. Could it be James?

Hooking his lantern to a protruding twig, Nicholas began to scramble cautiously down the side of the ditch, holding on to rough clumps of grass and mounds of earth. With limited light he could hardly see where to place his foot for his next downward step. Suddenly a loose stone gave way, and he found himself sliding helplessly into the ditch. He lay still for a moment at the bottom, dazed and shaken. Then, heart beating heavily, he began to grope around him. Suddenly he touched something. A man was lying prostrate almost beside him, with one leg doubled up under him. He appeared to be only semi-conscious.

Nicholas could just make out the grey jacket, black breeches and hose of a Royalist cavalryman. At that moment the moon emerged from behind a cloud. Now he could see the man's pallid face, drawn with pain; a tuft of fair hair plastered with blood was lying dankly across his forehead. As the farmer tried to make out the injured man's features, he could see that he was young, perhaps not much older than sixteen-year-old James. He must have been thrown from his horse as he hurtled across the rough ground, trying to escape the approaching horsemen.

But what could Nicholas do at this time of night? He could not possibly move the injured man on his own. And what about James? Why not leave this Royalist soldier to die? After all, who could tell what destruction he might already have wreaked on the properties, or even the persons, of innocent villagers? Nicholas hesitated, struggling with competing thoughts of anger, fear and pity.

A wounded cavalier

'Water,' whispered a hoarse voice, 'Water'.

'I must help him,' thought Nicholas frantically. What if it had been James lying there? 'I have no water,' he answered steadily, 'but I will go and fetch help.'

Reaching home he called his younger son, fourteen-year-old Robert, still awake and troubled about his brother, and then begged the help of two grumbling neighbours who unwillingly left their beds. After some persuasion the men agreed to help Nicholas. The party set off into the night, equipped with a rough coat to act as a makeshift stretcher.

Arriving at the spot, they scrambled down the bank, then slowly and with much difficulty managed to roll the injured soldier onto the coat, trying not to cause him undue distress. Each taking a corner, they staggered along the bottom of the rhyne with their burden until they reached a place where the slope of the bank was less steep. Here, breathless and exhausted, they rested until with one last effort they finally reached level ground. Groaning at first at every jolt along the way, the man had finally lapsed into unconsciousness and lay still and silent as Nicholas and his neighbours at last laid him down on the kitchen floor in Moorside Farm.

Thanking his friends sincerely for their help, Nicholas set off once more into the night to continue searching for his older son. Alice gazed helplessly at the soldier's still white face and blood-stained clothes. Was he already dead? She hardly knew. Breathing an urgent prayer to God for help, she fetched some warm water in a basin, and tried to bathe the ugly wound on his head and face. But his leg, still doubled up under him, was clearly badly broken.

When Nicholas at last returned in the early hours of the morning he looked tired and hopeless. Even though he had called his son's name repeatedly, he had neither seen nor heard any sign of him. Determined to continue his search at first light of day, he crossed the kitchen floor and gazed at the injured soldier lying near the stove. He was still unconscious, but Alice had managed to force a few drops of warm milk into his mouth and had bathed his wounds. The deep cuts on his face made Nicholas shudder. A wave of panic swept over him. What had he done in rescuing this youth? Who was he? How badly hurt? One thing was clear: if he should still be alive in the morning, something must be done about his damaged leg.

Nicholas and Alice were poor; they found it hard enough to scrape a meagre living from their sheep farm for themselves and their boys. Who then would pay for expensive medical care for this stranger? And, above all, where was James? As these perplexing questions swirled round his tired mind, Nicholas sunk down into a chair, and before long slept from sheer exhaustion.

As the first early rays of dawn broke across the moors, lighting up the kitchen, Nicholas woke and, after taking a little refreshment, set off to resume his search. Meanwhile Alice was left alone with her son Robert and an unknown soldier lying in the corner of the kitchen. A sensitive but practical woman, her hair now showing the first streaks of grey as she approached her forty-second birthday, Alice tried to put her personal fears to the back of her mind, as she pondered the best course of action. She must get medical help as soon as possible.

A slight sound attracted her attention. The young man appeared to be regaining consciousness. Crossing over to him with a cup of milk in her hand, she realized that he was trying to say something. 'Who are you?' she asked.

The only reply was a rasping sound; then Alice thought he was trying to say 'Wilm', but it was so indistinct that she was unsure whether she had heard aright. 'Wilm' — or perhaps it was 'Will' — was very young, his fresh, boyish features badly defaced by his wounds. Propping him up as best she could, Alice gave him a further drink, then laid him down gently.

At last Nicholas was back, his face grey and strained. He had just received news that a number of local men had been killed and wounded by the stampede of desperate cavalry escaping for their lives from Cromwell's pursuing army. Could his own boy be among them? James had been out rounding up the sheep at the very moment the horsemen had passed Moorside. Sick with fear, Nicholas had returned to tell Alice that he was about to saddle his horse and ride to the town hall at Langport where the casualties, both the dead and wounded, had been taken.

Meanwhile Alice had to make some decision about the young man lying on their floor. The local barber-surgeon, Randolph Bilton, was the one to consult. In addition to cutting hair he also dealt with minor surgical emergencies: he would lance boils, extract teeth, even undertake amputations if necessary. The only alternative was the town physician, but his fees were exorbitant, far more than Nicholas and Alice could afford. Sending Robert out to call on Bilton, or Randy Cut-throat, as the locals called him behind his back, Alice tried to cook a little gruel for the wounded man, but her hands were trembling so violently that she gave up and sank down on her knees in that silent kitchen and begged the God in whom she trusted for strength to endure whatever might happen.

2.
At what cost?

'Is he dead?' whispered James.

'Dead? Who?' asked Nicholas in bewilderment as he gazed at his son, lying helplessly at one end of a long table in the town hall. All around lay rows of injured men, Royalist and New Model Army men, but also a few locals and even a small child. A physician was walking up and down the rows, trying to assess each case. Some were clearly beyond hope, others more lightly injured.

'Who?' repeated Nicholas.

'… in the rhyne … his horse bolted…' The boy's voice was growing weaker. 'I did try, Papa… I did… It wasn't his fault… Oh, Papa…!' The words were becoming incoherent now. James was gradually slipping away and Nicholas knew it. Then the whole fearful scene flashed before the father's eyes: the bolting horse … his son's attempt to grab the reins … the boy dragged to the ground … the rider flung headlong into the ditch … oncoming horses trampling the boy as he lay prostrate on the path…

It was all so clear. Nicholas sat beside James, head in hands, for a few moments; then, rising heavily, he crossed over to where the physician was standing and begged his urgent help. But when he returned one glance told him that it was too late. Without doubt his eldest son had gone beyond recall. After a few further words with the physician, Nicholas, now almost paralysed with shock and grief, left the hall and struggled to mount his horse. Unable even to hold the reins steadily, he could only sit with glazed eyes, leaving the animal to find its own way home.

As Nicholas reached Moorside, he was surprised to see a stranger's horse — an ill-looking animal — tethered at the door. Entering the kitchen, he noticed his son Robert in one corner standing flat against the wall. Alice, with her back to the door, was talking to someone whose voice he recognized instantly, Randolph Bilton, the barber-surgeon. He just caught the tail end of the conversation. 'I am sorry to tell you, Madam Wilkes,' Bilton was saying, 'but there is nothing for it but to amputate the leg.' A large, uncouth-looking man, with a severe squint in one eye, Randolph Bilton had been examining the cavalryman's badly broken leg and was now pronouncing his verdict.

Alice shuddered. 'Surely not!' she cried. 'He's only young.' Then she caught sight of her husband standing in the doorway.

'You will do nothing of the sort, Master Bilton — at least not yet,' interrupted Nicholas abruptly, 'and I will ask you kindly to help me lift this man into a chair.' Bilton shrugged and replaced the rusty-looking saw he had produced from his bag of tools. Together the two men lifted the injured rider onto a chair. The youth's face was twisted with pain as they moved him, but he made no sound. 'And now I would ask you kindly to leave, and here are a couple of shillings for your pains.' Bilton accepted the coins, but swore under his breath — an amputation would have been worth at least a pound.[1] Then he shuffled out of the door and rode off.

Nicholas did not have to tell Alice that James was dead. She knew from his face. And as he repeated their son's last words, both turned instinctively and looked at the young man seated nearby. He had heard, and shook his head in silent grief. Bright tears gleamed in his eyes. 'Was he your boy?' he managed to say at last. Nicholas did not answer. Instead he turned to the speaker and asked directly, 'What is your name, young man?' Now able to speak a little more clearly, the youth replied, 'Wilmot, Hugh Wilmot.'

'Wilmot?' Both Nicholas and Alice gasped in shocked surprise. The name was a household word in the West Country. There could be few who had not heard of Lord Henry Wilmot, scourge of the parliamentary forces in the west before the creation of the New Model Army. Noticing their dismay, the young soldier whispered, 'Not my father, just my uncle.' Clearly shaken by the revelation of the young man's identity, Nicholas and Alice had a pressing decision to make. 'For James's sake we must get a second opinion on this injury,' said Alice in a voice shaking with emotion, for she was scarcely able to take in the enormity of her bereavement.

'We will speak of this later,' Nicholas responded sharply, with a sideways glance at Hugh Wilmot. Clearly the youth was in much pain: delay in his treatment could lead to gangrene and death. Faint with loss of blood and with little nourishment to sustain him, he appeared about to lose consciousness once more. Alice encouraged him to swallow a little warm broth before Robert and Nicholas lifted him as gently as they could and laid him on James's bed in a small room at the back of the farmhouse.

With Hugh Wilmot out of earshot, and minds numbed by their own loss, Nicholas, his wife and son Robert sat down to a frugal meal before discussing the predicament before them. 'How can we afford a physician's fees?' asked Nicholas. 'Our yearly produce of wool and mutton would hardly be enough to cover them, and we already face the funeral costs.'

'We could sell the cow,' chipped in Robert unexpectedly.

'Sell the cow?' repeated his father in astonishment. 'Sell the cow? But we need the milk she gives.'

'Not as much as that man needs his leg,' stated Robert doggedly.

'For James's sake,' repeated Alice softly, who almost saw such a gesture as a memorial for the son they had lost.

'But how can we do such a thing for an enemy? Think of all the death and destruction this boy's uncle has brought to our towns and villages!' objected Nicholas, as the memory of his son's poor broken body flashed across his mind. Lord Henry Wilmot! Just two years earlier that very man had led his forces in the assault on the Parliamentary army at nearby Roundway Down. His victory had brought the entire west of the country firmly under the king's banner. Taunton had later been devastated by fire. Though they understood that Wilmot was now in jail, having fallen from the king's favour for attempting to negotiate peace terms with the Earl of Essex, Lord-General of the Parliamentary army, his very name still instilled fear into the community.

'For James's sake we must help this man,' repeated Alice once again.

Nicholas did not reply. Rising to his feet, he merely said, 'I go to Langport.'

'May I come with you, Papa?' asked Robert.

'No, son. You must stay with your mother; she needs you,' replied his father steadily. Then he was gone. Alice knew he had made up his mind.

Two long hours crept past before Alice heard the clatter of horses' hooves approaching Moorside. Smoothing her apron and sweeping her long hair back from her face, Alice hurried to the door. As Samuel Atkins, the local physician, stooped to enter the low doorway, Alice hurried forward to greet him. Behind him, twisting his hands together nervously, stood Nicholas. 'Pleased to meet you, ma'am,' said the tall physician courteously. 'And where may I find the patient?'

A tense half-hour followed, as Atkins twisted and turned Wilmot's injured leg thoughtfully. Hugh winced in pain at each movement. Then at last the physician spoke. 'A serious break, young man,' he said, 'a very serious break. The bone is fractured in a number of places. I may indeed be able to set it, but I fear you will never fully regain the use of the leg. The only alternative is amputation, but that I would not recommend, unless all else fails.'

Hugh could only nod, and say at last, 'I thank you indeed for your kindness, sir, but I cannot pay. My parents are dead, and my uncle lies in jail.'

The physician glanced around the sparse room, then at Nicholas and Alice. 'My fees are high,' he said ruefully, 'and if I make concessions for one, then I must make them for all. Many were wounded in the stampede... Your own son, I believe...'

Nicholas swallowed hard. 'We will pay, sir,' he said abruptly.

'But he also needs much repair to those open wounds on his face. Should infection set in, his days will be but short. And how can you raise the five pounds that I must charge?'

'Do not fear, sir, you will be paid,' replied Nicholas slowly, 'for I have a handsome cow, an excellent milker, which will fetch a fair price at auction next week.'

'I will return shortly with my assistant,' said Atkins, shaking Nicholas' hand warmly. And then, almost as an afterthought, he added kindly, 'And may the God in whom you trust comfort you for the loss of your brave son, and reward you for your mercy to a stranger.'

Saddling his horse, Samuel Atkins rode away.

3.
How can I forgive?

When Hugh Wilmot limped off into the early morning mist of an October day in 1645, Alice and Nicholas felt an unexpected wave of sadness. The nearby woods glowed with the bronzes and golds of autumn; the distant river gleamed in the early sunlight. Yet a brooding gloom seemed to hang over the landscape — a sense of uncertainty, of approaching winter days, with a strange foreboding of an unknown future.

Hugh had stoically borne the agony as Samuel Atkins set his broken leg, while his assistant held the young man down in case the pain became intolerable. But the stitching on his face had caused him the most distress. Alice had left the room, unable any longer to endure the trauma of hearing the patient's subdued moans as Atkins attempted to repair the deep wounds across his left cheek and forehead — a process carried out with only a whiff of opiate to dull the pain.

A typical Somerset farm

To her had fallen the task of caring for the invalid during the six long weeks that it had taken for his leg, fastened firmly between two splints, to heal. Day after day she tried to tempt him back to health with the best meals she could afford, for now the family resources were low following the sale of the cow. Any milk they needed had to be purchased from neighbouring farms. To some extent the care of the young man had eased Alice's acute pain at the loss of her own son. Yet Hugh was surprisingly uncommunicative — even unresponsive — in spite of all the kindness shown to him.

Something was wrong, and it was not just the confinement and discomfort, for his youthful strength was gradually returning. Then one day he spoke. Each morning Nicholas was in the habit of reading aloud a passage of Scripture before he began his day's work on the farm, and each morning Hugh listened in the same sullen silence. But then things changed. The passage Nicholas chose that day was the account of the crucifixion of Christ:

> And when they were come to the place, which is called Calvary, there they crucified him, and the malefactors, one on the right hand, and the other on the left. Then said Jesus, Father, forgive them; for they know not what they do.[1]

Suddenly there was a strange choking sound from the chair where Hugh was seated, one leg stretched out resting on a small stool in front of him.

'How can I forgive?' he cried angrily. 'How can I?' All eyes turned towards the speaker. 'No never,' he added with a determined shake of his head.

'Why do you speak so?' asked Nicholas with a hint of reproof in his voice.

Then it all came out in a rush: 'Two years ago I saw my own father, all I had and loved in this world — hacked to death, he was, at Roundway Down by a vicious parliamentary soldier.' He gulped back tears and then continued. 'I was following hard behind him and saw him fall from his horse, wounded but not fatally. Why then add blow to blow and kill him?' demanded Hugh viciously, 'Why?' He lapsed into silence, then went on: 'I stayed with him until the end, while the battle raged forward. And I vowed I would live to avenge his death... It would be my goal in life... Then your boy tried to save me as my horse reared up in terror at some phantom in the darkness ... and you ... you took me in and ... and... So how can I fulfil my mission of vengeance now?' he ended lamely.

Hugh began to sob like a child. Nicholas and Robert tactfully left the room, while Alice remained until Hugh

had calmed down. Only seventeen years of age, he had
come to love Alice like the mother he had never known,
but even she had been unable to penetrate the barrier of
reserve that Hugh had erected like a wall between them.
Now she understood.

A tense silence followed — words seemed inappropri-
ate at that moment. But in the days that followed Hugh
spoke much of his childhood, of his passionate interest in
all living things, of his faint memories of his mother, of the
bond with his father, of his hatred of cruelty, of his horror
at a war dividing and destroying families for ever, of his
fear and dislike of his uncle and his determination to
search out his father's killer… Although Alice spoke gently
to the troubled youth of the compassion of God towards
his enemies, and his mercy to the penitent through Christ,
Hugh seemed unable to understand.

But it was to Robert that he was able to speak most
freely. While Alice was busy about the house and Nicholas
cared for the farm, the two chatted together. Hugh told the
admiring boy strange tales of court life, of places he had
visited, even of the embattled king, Charles I, and his
dashing nephew, the handsome Prince Rupert of the
Rhine. It made Robert's life seem dull by comparison. The
younger boy secretly determined that one day he would
leave the quiet rural existence he had known — he would
travel; he would fight; he would make a name for himself.

Then one day a messenger arrived at Moorside Farm
astride a splendid white mare. Tethering the animal to the
fence, he knocked loudly on the kitchen door. News of
Hugh Wilmot's whereabouts, carried by word of mouth
first to one and then to another, had finally filtered through
to his uncle, Lord Henry Wilmot. He heard of his nephew's

brush with death, of his severe wounds, of his rescue and the generosity of a poor farmer and his wife. Recently released from Exeter Jail himself, Wilmot had fled to France, where he was presently serving out a period of exile in the court of Queen Henrietta Maria, wife of Charles I.

Now he was sending for Hugh to come to him as soon as he had recovered sufficiently from his injuries. The messenger, one whom Hugh recognized as his uncle's trusted valet, was about to leave when he placed a small packet on the kitchen table, thanked Alice and Nicholas for their services to his master's nephew and then rode off. To their astonishment, the packet contained ten shining gold sovereigns[2] — enough to purchase another cow, to compensate for any expenses they had incurred and to provide a fund for any future needs.

Two days later Hugh announced that he was well enough to leave. The ugly cuts on his face were healing well, but he would be scarred for life; one leg was distinctly shorter than the other, so that he would never regain that fine physique he had before. But despite the injuries he had never complained. Perhaps it was Robert who felt the greatest sense of loss as Hugh Wilmot thanked Nicholas and Alice sincerely for all their kindness and set off for the nearby village of Huish Episcopi, adjacent to Langport, that October morning. He had arranged to meet his uncle's valet in the porch of the grand old village church and travel with him to France.

Robert looked after the figure of his new friend as he disappeared, limping, into the distance. The two had become increasingly close in recent weeks. Something about the younger boy's love of fun, his generous if impulsive nature, appealed to Hugh. Robert, for his part, now nearing his fifteenth birthday, had found in Hugh one whom he admired intensely for his courage, his powers of endurance, his refusal to be broken by adverse circumstances. Even Hugh's stubborn strength of mind had a strange appeal.

'We shall miss you, Hugh,' said Robert simply, just before Hugh left. 'I fear we shall never meet again.'

Turning serious blue eyes on the boy, Hugh replied, 'Who can tell? And one day, perhaps I can repay you for your kindness and for the loss of your brother's life.' With these words he turned away quickly, hiding the emotion welling up inside him. In a few moments he had gone from sight.

4.
THE PAST EXPLAINED

Moorside Farm seemed strangely empty as life resumed its normal routine once more. The gap left by James's death now hit each of them intensely, but in a different way. Nicholas had been relying on his older son to take over the farm, relieving him of the daily burden and worry. A reliable and steady young man, James had been a complete contrast to Robert, who often seemed irresponsible and disinterested in the routine of farm life. Nicholas reacted to his bereavement by retreating into a troubled silence as his mind went over and over the sad train of circumstances leading to his son's death. Had he been responsible? He had sent James on a mission which placed him — unintentionally, it was true — in harm's way. For the safety of a few sheep he had put his son's life at risk... What had he done? If only...!

A passage of Scripture kept drumming in the back of Nicholas' mind — one that was pointed out to him by Francis Bartlett, the acknowledged leader of the small group of men and women who met together each Sunday in Langport to read the Bible, talk and pray together. 'The secret things belong unto the LORD our God', it said, and then something about 'those things that are revealed…',[1] but Nicholas could not remember the rest. 'Was this tragedy one of God's "secret things"?', he thought heavily. If so, he must stop demanding explanations and believe that somehow, somewhere, God had a secret purpose in those events and one day he would understand. Nicholas had searched for the words in his tattered copy of the Bible, which he had been able to purchase several years earlier on a market stall, but had not been able to find them. He must remember to ask Francis Bartlett about them when they next met.

Alice, meanwhile, though equally desolate at the loss of James, seemed more able to find acceptance and peace than Nicholas. Her life had been far from easy in the early years. Born in 1604 in Enfield, a village just north of London, Alice was the elder of two girls. Her father had shown her little affection: he had wanted a son, and nothing Alice could do seemed to please him. Sometimes he would strike her viciously even for minor offences, leaving his daughter bruised and frightened. Her sister, Ruth, on the other hand, petite and dark-haired, had always been her father's favourite, and although the two girls had remained firm friends, Alice had fought long against a sense of rejection. Her mother, clearly afraid of her husband, had died in a smallpox epidemic that had spread through the community when Alice was only eleven. This event, coupled with her father's hasty remarriage only three months later, was decisive for the girl. She would leave home as soon as she was old enough. The following year she managed to find employment as a kitchen maid in the household of a merchant in nearby Barnet, John Tillman and his wife Mary.

To Alice's mind her new master had some strange religious views. Instead of attending the parish church each Sunday, he would sling his best cloak over his shoulders, mount his horse, with his wife riding pillion, and make his way right across London, over London Bridge, to attend a meeting place in Southwark. Apparently he belonged to a group of men and women known as Separatists or Independents. Convinced that the true church consisted only of those whose lives had been transformed by faith in Christ, these men and women were unhappy about worshipping in the parish churches under clergy, many of whom had little or no faith.

Alice did not trouble her head too much about such things, but it was the kindness of his wife, Mary, that affected her deeply. Not many years older than Alice herself, Mary Tillman often spoke to the girl: she knew of her unhappy home life and would tell her tenderly of a God who is a merciful Father to his people, one in whom she could always find a refuge, and whose love would never fail her. She spoke too of a Saviour in Christ who had borne untold suffering and death that sinners might find forgiveness.

Alice found it hard to grasp such ideas, but gradually over the years she responded to all that her mistress told her, and found a peace and consolation in God through Jesus Christ and an assurance of forgiveness for the many wrongs which had often troubled her. Now she listened with interest to all that John Tillman told her of the church he attended in Southwark, of his pastor John Lathrop, of the spiritual convictions that gave these people courage to suffer for their beliefs. He told her of the increasing hostility towards such churches by a government that insisted on uniformity of religious belief throughout the country and regular attendance at a state parish church. Occasionally Alice even travelled with the family on a Sunday when her duties permitted. And it was there she first met Nicholas — a tall, dark-haired farmer's son with a strange thick accent and an infectious laugh. Apparently he was from the West Country, but what he was doing in London, she never asked. Although he was some years older than Alice, she knew that he had noticed her as she sat shyly at the back of the meeting house, and had even made a point of helping her back onto her horse after the services were over.

As time passed Alice became concerned about her father. True, he had shown her no love, but when she heard from her younger sister, Ruth, that their father was unwell and neglected by his second wife, she knew she must visit him. Ruth herself was due to be married shortly to a merchant from Wellington, in Somerset, whom she had met while he was on business in London. When Alice saw the state of the home and her father's emaciated condition, she was appalled and decided with regret that she must terminate her employment with the Tillman family and return home to care for the bad-tempered old man.

With a tenderness that at first surprised him and then gradually softened and won his affection, Alice did all in her power to ease the suffering of her father's last years. Lonely, depressed and forsaken by his wife, he clung tenaciously to his elder daughter for his happiness.

After his death two years later, Alice decided that the time had come for her to leave London for good. Where could she go? Recently she had found herself thinking about the young man she had met briefly at Southwark more than two years earlier, but apart from knowing that his home had been in the West Country, she had no idea where he could be by now.

While she was wondering what to do, an urgent message arrived for Alice from her sister Ruth's husband. Ruth, he told her, had recently given birth to twins, and was far from well. Would it be possible for Alice to come and care for the home until Ruth was stronger? Delighted at the thought of time with her sister and the babies, Alice packed a few possessions and enquired about a passage on a carriage travelling west.

Before she left she decided to visit the Tillman family, first to tell them of her father's death and also to say a last goodbye. But secretly Alice had another motive for her visit. She would enquire, as carefully as she could, whether her former employer knew anything of Nicholas Wilkes.

'Nicholas? Nicholas Wilkes?' boomed John Tillman with a hearty laugh. 'Why, gone back home, as far as I know. London life did not suit him — a country lad, born and bred.'

'And where would that be?' asked Alice, blushing — her interest a little too obvious.

'Why, Somerset way, I believe; near Taunton, if I remember rightly,' replied John with a knowing chuckle. Now twenty-two, Alice was a beautiful young woman, her long fair hair framing the fine features of a sensitive face. Only her work-roughened hands told another story. 'Aye, he's a good lad is Nicholas,' John added as an afterthought.

Moorland landscape

'Only you mind you don't forget the words of the Bible — remember it says, "Delight thyself also in the LORD; and he shall give thee the desires of thine heart." '[2]

Alice was used to her former employer quoting Scripture to her so she merely smiled shyly and said, 'I won't forget.'

Three months later, with her sister Ruth well on the way to recovery, Alice decided to stay in that area. She loved walking on the open moorland and, with no other living relatives apart from her sister, it seemed a wise decision. Before long she found a job helping at the Taunton cattle market. For a town girl Alice was surprisingly adept at dealing with animals, and loved her job. She resolutely put Nicholas Wilkes out of her mind: the chances that she would ever see him again were indeed remote.

Twice weekly the farmers from all the surrounding area brought their animals for sale by auction and it was Nicholas who first spotted Alice while he was standing on the outskirts of the crowd waiting to pen his sheep. He noticed the fair-haired woman bending over one of the pens, fastening the latch. She reminded him of someone, and he was not quite sure who. But as soon as she straightened and glanced in his direction he knew: it was the same girl that he had seen at Southwark almost three years earlier.

Nicholas, a highly able youth, had left the family farm hoping to make money in the city through the wool trade. But circumstances were adverse for such a venture at the time, and eventually he had returned home bitterly disappointed over the failure of his business endeavours. But he was not the loser, for during his time under the preaching of John Lathrop he had found a treasure of far greater worth — the grace of God to sinners.

Delighted to see Alice again, Nicholas lost no time in arranging to meet up with her after her duties were complete. Once again his infectious laugh and broad, gruff accent intrigued Alice, but a greater bond now drew them together as they shared a common faith and even a willingness to suffer for Christ's sake if necessary. In 1627, with Alice now twenty-three and Nicholas almost thirty, they were married in a simple ceremony conducted by Francis Bartlett in a small meeting room hired for the occasion in the nearby town of Langport.

Later that day — for no farmer could spare time for a honeymoon — Alice was gladly welcomed to Moorside Farm where Nicholas, whose parents had recently died, had been managing on his own. With evidence of a bachelor's lifestyle all around, Alice set to work to turn the old farmhouse into a home. At last she knew the joy of being both loved and wanted.

When their boys were born, James in 1629 and Robert in 1632, Alice and Nicholas had little idea that, far off in London, a situation was developing between King Charles I and his Parliament which would eventually plunge the whole country into a fearful war and profoundly affect their own lives. But they did discover an increasing measure of intolerance towards those who, like themselves, wished to worship God in freedom of conscience independently of the national church. Rumours of torture and heavy fines instigated by Archbishop William Laud against such people were the talk of the marketplace when Nicholas took his sheep for auction in Taunton. Some of their friends were even thinking about emigrating to the New World in search of the right to worship without state interference.

Alice worried about the future for her young sons. Then in 1642, when James was thirteen, hostilities erupted as the king raised his standard in Nottingham, and men of all ages were enlisted to march to battle, some for the king, some for Parliament. Boys as young as sixteen were recruited to fight, and many were to die for competing ideals. And it was this war that would lead to James's death and Hugh Wilmot's injuries — two young men, two opposing sides, but one tragedy.

5.
LOSSES AND GAINS

Robert was restless. He missed Hugh at every turn — missed his enthralling stories and his cheerful spirit in spite of the obvious pain of his injuries. But most of all Robert missed James. His older brother had been a constant foil against Robert's erratic behaviour. Again and again when Nicholas discovered that his younger son had failed once more either to obey him or to undertake some task, James would think of some excuse for his brother, or even take the blame himself. A highly intelligent boy, Robert seemed content only when he could steal away to some hidden corner of the farm and immerse himself in a book, perhaps a tale of high adventure or of daring exploits of the past. Engrossed in his book, he seemed oblivious to time. Sometimes he would be following the exploits of Don Quixote, or be trembling with fear as Banquo's ghost returns to haunt Macbeth for the vile murders he has committed.

Alice often sighed as she looked at her son, now almost fifteen. He showed so little interest in the farm and, with James gone, she wondered how Nicholas would cope with all the burden of work that fell to him. Maybe, she thought, Robert would begin to see that his own interests were tied up with the farm and change his ways now that James was no longer there. But it was not so. If anything the boy became more moody, less co-operative and seemed unaware of his parents' pain and need.

Sundays were the most difficult of all. The principles and truths that Alice and Nicholas held dear meant little to Robert. Why his parents could not attend the parish church like everyone else was more than he could understand — it isolated him from the only social contact he had with the other village boys in Langport, those he had known when they had attended the village school together. Instead Alice and Nicholas would hitch the pony to the farm wagon each week and join a small group of other men and women meeting in the home of Francis Bartlett — a man whom Nicholas had known since the days when they both listened to the preaching of John Lathrop in Southwark.

Robert always tried to sit in some corner where the tall, ginger-haired preacher could not see him, but it usually proved impossible. His searching, earnest eyes seemed to penetrate Robert's inner thoughts wherever he sat. However much he might try to avoid Master Bartlett, Robert could not escape his own thoughts and the conviction that one day he must face up to the truths he was hearing so repeatedly. But for now he erected fresh barriers in his mind. Why did James have to die like that? Why was Hugh so terribly injured? What was the war about anyway? And why should religion always divide people as it did?

There seemed to be no easy answers to Robert's questions, nor did he feel able to share his concerns with anyone. As the months passed he became less and less helpful to his parents even though he could see them visibly ageing. At last, when the youth reached the age of sixteen, his father could stand it no longer. Accosting his son as he loitered around the farm one day, Nicholas put an ultimatum to him: either the boy must change his attitudes and see that his future lay in the farm, that his father needed him, needed his clear thinking mind and abilities, or he must leave home and make his own way in life. He had to decide. Robert chose the latter.

Nicholas still had contacts in London, associates whom he had known when he had tried unsuccessfully to develop a business in the wool trade. Then he had an idea. Why not approach his former friend, Bernard Allen, who had set himself up in printing and publishing? With Robert's overriding interest in books and learning, Bernard might now be in a position to take on an apprentice and instruct him in the book trade. True, the days had been difficult for every publisher as a result of the strict censorship laws imposed on all publications by the government of Charles I and his former archbishop, William Laud. But with Laud now executed and the Puritan Parliament in control, restrictions had been eased.

Robert responded enthusiastically to the suggestion and in 1647 accompanied his father to Old Broad Street, near Bishop's Gate, just outside the old city wall of London. There, shining in the early spring sunshine, they saw a notice hanging over the doorway of a three-storey building that read:

Sign of the Morning Star
Bernard Allen
Publisher

And, sure enough, there they found Bernard Allen himself, busy setting up the typeface for a pamphlet he was producing. Flustered and overworked, Bernard scarcely had time to greet his old friend, but when he heard the purpose of the visit, a slow smile spread across his face. 'Why!' he exclaimed in his broad Somerset accent, for he was a fellow West Country man, 'if that isn't just what I wanted!' He turned his gaze on Robert, who felt himself reddening under Master Allen's eyes. Tall like his father and fair like Alice, Robert was a well-built young man with strong masculine features and bright, intelligent eyes. Bernard nodded slowly. 'And when would you like him to start?' he asked Nicholas.

'We must talk business,' said Nicholas, as the two disappeared together into a back room. Apprentices were normally indentured to their masters for a seven-year period by a legal agreement, and Nicholas would be required to pay either a lump sum or alternatively an annual fee in return for his son's board, clothing and training. While the two were discussing mutually agree-able terms, Robert was left to wander round the workshop, examining the presses, inks and piles of printed sheets, ready to be folded, sewn and bound.

Suddenly a slight noise startled him. Looking up, he had a quick glimpse of a young girl's face peering cheekily round the door. She had disappeared in a moment, leaving Robert to wonder whether his imagination had been tricking him. Perhaps she was a kitchen maid, thought the boy, and dismissed her from his mind. At that moment Nicholas and Bernard reappeared, having reached a settlement. Unable to afford the seven-year fee in advance, Nicholas had agreed to pay three pounds annually to Bernard. As Bernard was clearly under some pressure, Nicholas and Robert soon left. In a month's time Robert would return, fee in hand, to begin a new life.

However, Robert's departure left Nicholas and Alice heavy-hearted. Not only had they lost James, but their younger son had also moved away for good. Nicholas now had even less assistance on the farm. With the sheep to be gathered from the moor, the demanding shearing routine, fleeces to be rolled and bundled up ready for sale, animals to be taken to Taunton Market for auction, together with all the day-to-day responsibilities of the farm and the pressures of the lambing season, Nicholas soon realized that he could not manage on his own. Now almost fifty years of age, he urgently needed help.

The first young man he employed proved untrust-worthy. Small sums of money began to disappear until at last Nicholas was obliged to dismiss him in disgrace. The second was reliable enough but too clumsy, too inept for the work. For some months Nicholas toiled on unaided, but day by day he prayed that he might find someone suitable who could help him. Most young men were still caught up in the army, as a second civil war had broken out, embroil-ing parts of the country in bloodshed once more. When would these things end, sighed Nicholas, as he thought of youths like Hugh Wilmot maimed for life, or killed like his own son, James. Why could king, army and Parliament not agree amicable terms for ruling the country?

Then, one bitterly cold night early in 1648, a strange sound was heard in the lane outside the farm. Was someone calling for help? Jumping up, Nicholas strained to look into the darkness but could see nothing. Nervously Alice continued to fill the stone bottles with hot water ready to warm the bed. Then both were startled by a faint knock on the window. Cautiously Nicholas opened the back door a little and looked this way and that. Still he saw nothing. Just as he was about to close the door once more he thought he noticed a movement beside a nearby bush. Slowly, hesitantly, a figure rose and staggered towards him. Stupefied with surprise, Nicholas was about to slam the door shut when he saw it was an elderly man — a man in desperate need. Hastily Nicholas stepped outside and helped the stranger into the warm, where he sat him down on a kitchen chair. Alice offered him a bowl of soup and later a bed for the night — all these were customary courtesies to be given to any wayfaring traveller. Explanations could wait until the morning.

And an alarming tale it was. Walter Bayes had been forced out of his home on the outskirts of Martock by a handful of ruthless and desperate men waving rough batons. Former mercenaries, these men had been employed to fight for the Royalist cause against the Parliamentary army, or Roundheads as they were known. With their unit now disbanded, these ex-soldiers had been roaming the countryside looking for food and shelter, often brutalizing defenceless villagers. Robbed, beaten up and forced out into the night, Walter Bayes had fallen on the path from shock and weakness. Then he realized that unless he tried to reach refuge he would perish in the cold.

A moorland farm track

'Since my wife died two years ago, I have lived alone,' he told Nicholas and Alice. 'What could I do against such villains?' Perhaps he could reach his son's home in Pibsbury, near Langport, some six miles across the moor. It was his only hope. If he followed the course of the River Parrett it might be possible to find his way despite the dark and mist. But, weak and dazed, Walter had become hopelessly lost. Almost at the point of collapse, he had seen a light shining from the window of Moorside Farm.

Not surprisingly, their elderly visitor was far from well the following day and in no condition to be moved even to nearby Pibsbury. Grateful to Alice for her kind invitation to stay until he was stronger, Walter Bayes told his new friends of his past life. To their astonishment they learned that he had once been Sir John Digby's chief herdsman at Sherborne Lodge. Situated not far from Yeovil, the magnificent home had been built by the unfortunate Sir Walter Raleigh before he was eventually executed under Elizabeth I's successor, James I. After his death the mansion had passed into the possession of the Digby family.

Although there was little that Walter Bayes did not know about sheep, and Sir John's flocks had become second to none in the area, Bayes had been abruptly dismissed at the outbreak of the Civil War in 1642 when Sir John Digby, a strong Royalist, discovered that his herdsman had Puritan sympathies. Since then the days had been hard for Walter, with the recent death of his wife leaving him bereft and friendless.

That night Nicholas spoke privately to Alice. True, Walter Bayes was elderly, but surely this was the answer to his many prayers. Here was someone brought so unexpectedly to their very door whose knowledge of sheep and sheep-farming was greater than his own. Bayes had also told them that his son in nearby Pibsbury was an ardent Catholic and had little sympathy with his elderly father's views; he feared he would not be welcome there. Too afraid to return to his cottage in Marston, Bayes gratefully accepted the offer of a position at Moorside assisting Nicholas with the animals as much as he was able in return for his accommodation.

Walter Bayes was also happy to accompany Nicholas and Alice to the home of Master Bartlett and his wife Edith in Langport each Sunday. On the outskirts of the town, the Bartletts' home was almost under the shadow of the splendid but hostile church of St Mary's the Virgin, built on a small prominence and appearing to stand guard over the town. Often despised in the community, some of these men and women who met together with Nicholas and Alice had already suffered severely for their faith before the outbreak of civil war. But now, with Parliament in the ascendancy and Oliver Cromwell's broadminded views on religious toleration prevailing, the situation for Independents, or Dissenters as they were sometimes called, was easing.

With this greater degree of tolerance, the number of people crowding into the home of Francis and Edith each Sunday was growing steadily. The crush, especially on hot summer days, was becoming unbearable. A solution to the overcrowding must soon be found, and a decision was taken late in 1648 to build a more permanent meeting house where they could gather each week. Despite the new freedom for Independent churches, its leaders well knew that this might not last. Any location must therefore afford both protection and a quick escape route in case officious magistrates, stirred up by angry clerics, should interrupt their services, or even arrest members of the church as they had done before.

Nicholas had a suggestion. What better place could they find than somewhere in the woods overlooking the wild and barren reaches of West Sedgemoor? Crisscrossed as they were by deep and treacherous ditches and footpaths that petered out in scrubland, few would venture on the moors, especially after dark. Secret hideouts were plentiful if the need arose. Eventually a decision was made. Red Hill, little more than two miles from Moorside Farm, seemed the ideal spot. In a small natural clearing among the trees, building went ahead apace.

Simply constructed with strong timber-framed walls, wattle-and-daub panels and a thatched roof, the new meeting house was soon lined with sturdy benches for the worshippers and even a secret cupboard behind the pulpit where the preacher could hide if the need arose. Concealed there among the trees, the Independents of Langport could now meet together in comfort and with relative peace of mind.

6.
THE DAY THAT EVERYTHING CHANGED

The seventeen-year-old boy was standing impatiently on the outskirts of a vast crowd. The day was bitterly cold and Robert shivered, pulling his cloak more tightly around his shoulders. What was going on? He had an errand to fulfil and clearly would not be able to push his way through the crowd.

Almost twenty months had passed since Nicholas had brought his son to Old Broad Street at Bishop's Gate in the City of London and left him to begin his apprenticeship under the competent guidance of Bernard Allen. With a will to learn, Robert had quickly mastered the basic skills of setting the type by arranging the tiny copper letters in order, inking them and then winding down the heavy screw with a lever to put pressure onto the paper. Up went the screw again as the next sheet was inserted, while the

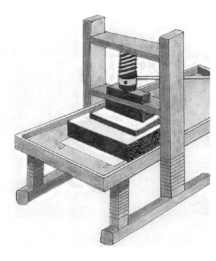

A seventeenth-century printing
press

first was drying. A long and tiresome business, it left Robert's arm aching at the end of a day's work.

That day Bernard Allen had asked his apprentice to carry proof sheets of a pamphlet he had printed to the author, who lived across the City in Great Peter Street, Westminster. Despite the cold Robert was glad of the break from the monotony of the workshop and decided to walk along the Thames riverbank even though it would take a little longer. He loved to watch the small boats hurrying up and down the busy waterway, their owners shouting greetings to each other as they passed.

But today things seemed different. A strange, tense hush rested over the city, and as Robert approached Whitehall he found himself hemmed in by a vast concourse of people. He could go no further. 'What's happening?' he asked someone who stood near him.

'They are executing our king,' came the terse reply.

'Executing our king?' echoed Robert in horror. He was aware that Charles I was in custody, that he was accused of 'treacherously and maliciously' waging war against Parliament and against his own people. Robert needed little reminder of the recent wars in which his own brother

James had been mown down in a stampede and Hugh Wilmot maimed for life… But could it possibly be right to put the king to death? Surely the king was appointed by God…? Then, above the heads of the crowd, he saw some-thing flash, swift as light, followed immediately by a sound he could never forget — a fearsome, agon-

King Charles I

ized groan from the crowd that seemed to travel in waves right over him.

'Such a groan as I never heard before, and desire I may never hear again,' he later recollected with a shudder. The king was dead. Robert had seen the fatal axe strike, sever-ing head from body. Dismay was written on every face around. A woman nearby fainted. Others wept. 30 January 1649 was a day that Englishmen would remember as a turning point in the history of their land.

Robert glanced around at the ashen-faced crowd. Everyone was hurrying away as though fearful of being personally implicated in a crime. Then, suddenly, some distance away on the far side of the crowd, Robert caught a glimpse of a face he recognized, a fair-haired young man with an ugly scar across his left cheek — Hugh, Hugh Wilmot! Threading his way urgently through the thinning crowd, Robert managed to reach the spot, but Hugh was nowhere to be seen. Where had he gone? Where? Robert never found out. But the sight awakened in him a longing to find Hugh — a desire that grew stronger with the passing days.

Confused and troubled, Robert fulfilled his errand and returned to Master Allen. He felt unable to mention what he had seen and heard, but the following day Bernard Allen informed his apprentice that the king had been executed. Then he added a strange remark: 'Perhaps now King Jesus will reign over this land.'

Robert could only nod dumbly, then leave the work-shop. Hurrying up the rickety stairs to his attic bedroom, he sat on his bed for a full half-hour reliving the whole dreadful scene of yesterday. Then he was startled by a soft knock on his door. He did not reply, but the door opened anyway and a dark-haired girl slipped in. Emma, Bernard Allen's only daughter, was shy and sensitive. Now four-teen, she was the one Robert had glimpsed briefly when he first came to Old Broad Street. With warm brown eyes and a gentle personality, she had appealed to Robert from the start. Somehow she seemed to understand him but, know-ing his position in the home as a mere apprentice, he had rarely spoken to her.

Emma said nothing, just pulled up a chair beside Robert. For a full five minutes they sat in silence. Then Robert blurted out suddenly, 'I saw it happen. It was terrible… And that groan…'

'I knew you had,' was all the girl replied, and then added, 'You must not grieve. You have suffered enough already. Perhaps these terrible wars will be over now.'

'Maybe,' Robert conceded. That was all. Then they lapsed into silence once more, until Emma rose to go. Her mother must never know she had been in Robert's room. Sarah Allen, a vivacious and strong-willed woman, had kept her three children, Emma and her young brothers, Timothy and Thomas — identical twins — firmly under control. The seven-year-old boys were bright and mischievous, and enjoyed playing tricks on Robert. They had welcomed him into the home like an older brother, but always there was a barrier between the apprentice and the family, one which often left Robert feeling a stranger.

Sundays were the most difficult of all. With little to do, Robert attended the church to which the family belonged. From early Sunday morning Robert could hear the steady tramp of feet past his window as men and women poured down Old Broad Street into Wormwood Street and on into Great St Helen's Street. Used to being among only a few worshippers in Master Bartlett's home, Robert was amazed to see almost a thousand people gathering to hear the preaching of a man with one of the strangest names he had ever heard, Hanserd Knollys.

When Robert attended he was not expected to sit with the Allen family, but at the back of the crowded meeting house. This did not worry him as he was able to look round at leisure on all the people gathered there, and most of all to survey the oddly named preacher. Formerly a minister of the established church in Lincolnshire, Knollys had become unhappy over certain practices such as the admission of unbelievers to communion service, so Robert had been told. He resigned his ministry, but continued to preach in local churches and as a result he had experienced much suffering. Robert heard that on one occasion his hearers had actually started to throw stones at him while he was preaching. A short time later Knollys fled to New England to avoid further persecution, returning in 1641 to care for his elderly father. In 1646, after a period as an

Hanserd Knollys

army chaplain in the Civil War, Knollys had gathered a congregation and started this Separatist church in Great St Helen's Street.

Even though Robert was secretly amused at the preacher's appearance, at the odd tufts of hair sticking out from under his tight-fitting black cap, he also found himself compelled to listen to some of the forthright and direct words he heard. Sometimes he thought that the preacher had spotted him at the back and was addressing his remarks directly at him. But, no, that could not be true, he told himself as he moved behind a tall middle-aged man and his plump wife, and was therefore well hidden from view.

However, Robert was not as careless about these things as he had once been. Ever since the execution of Charles I he often found himself thinking about death and eternity. The very word 'eternity' scared him. Then one day Hanserd Knollys said something which Robert found both disturbing and unforgettable. 'The great need you have of Christ may move you to prize him, and set a high esteem on him. Christ is the only thing necessary,' he declared. Yes, Robert certainly felt a great need, a sort of vacuum inside, but in his own mind he was sure that success and money were the answer, and managed to push the preacher's words to the back of his mind.

Although Sarah Allen ruled her home with a degree of severity which frightened Robert, she was not an unkind woman. She wished she could approach the young man who worked for her husband, but he appeared to erect a barrier around himself. She had also noticed that her daughter Emma seemed to watch Robert and was sometimes unduly attentive to his needs — something of which she strongly disapproved. Never should the daughter of a master printer, one of Bernard Allen's standing in society, be seen showing interest in an apprentice boy like Robert Wilkes. Yet she could not fault his conduct. What had escaped her attention was the number of times that Emma was busy shopping in the marketplace when Robert was out on an errand delivering proof sheets or finished copies from his master's printing presses.

In those brief moments when their paths crossed, Robert would talk to Emma as he could speak to no one else. He told her of his brother, James, of Hugh, of his ambitions, his uncertainties and even his spiritual fears. Emma herself, now almost seventeen, was becoming a beautiful young woman and Robert grappled against his rising affections. Although she was a good listener, she would also share her inmost thoughts. Then their ways would separate. Breathless and red-faced, Emma hurried home, always hoping that no neighbours had seen her talking to Robert.

Then the worst happened. Deep in conversation, Emma and Robert had failed to notice the cheeky faces of her ten-year-old twin brothers, Timothy and Thomas, or Tim and Tom as they were usually called, peering round a corner in Threadneedle Street. The boys could not wait to report what they had seen to their mother. Angrily Sarah Allen forbade her daughter to speak to the apprentice again, and even Bernard himself reproved Robert severely for taking such liberties with his only daughter.

Now twenty, and more than halfway through his apprenticeship, Robert was at a crossroads. A capable young man, he had become skilled at every aspect of printing, even carving out the wood cuttings to form the elaborate capital letters so often used at the beginning of a chapter. Unsettled and restless, he felt there was little left that Bernard Allen could teach him. Added to this, that fleeting glimpse of Hugh Wilmot three years earlier had affected him deeply. In recent months he had been carefully saving up any money that Bernard had paid him, for he could not quite give up the idea of eventually finding Hugh, though he realized that by now he must be mixing in far different circles from those of the farmer's son from Somerset. And then there was Emma.

At last he made a big decision.

7.
STOPPED IN HIS TRACKS

Early one morning in 1652 Robert crept from his attic room. In one hand he carried two carefully folded paper packets, in the other his few possessions, his clothes and a little food wrapped in a bundle. Around his waist he had tied a bag of coins — most of the money he had saved. No one else in the house was awake as the young man stealthily made his way down the stairs and into the workshop. On the larger of the two printing presses Robert laid one of his envelopes. Then he tiptoed into the kitchen, where Emma always hung her apron in readiness for the day's work. Into the pocket he slipped the other packet. Back to the front door he went, took down the large key hanging on a string nearby and opened the creaking door as quietly as he could. Then he was out. The cool morning air struck him full in the face as he strode off down Old Broad Street, without daring to look back even for a moment.

When Bernard Allen entered his workshop shortly after seven that morning he fully expected to find Robert already at work. Important parliamentary documents were to be printed that day to complete a contract that Bernard had recently obtained. But where was the boy? Annoyed, Bernard called to him from the bottom of the stairs. No reply. Then he became concerned. Could anything have happened? Certainly he had not had this trouble before, but his apprentice had seemed moody of late.

Hurrying up the stairs two at a time, he knocked loudly on Robert's door. When he received no answer he burst into the room. It was empty, stripped of personal possessions, the bed neatly made. Then the truth began to dawn on him. Robert had gone. Only when he returned to the workshop did he notice the packet on the press. As he unfolded it, two gold sovereigns rolled onto the floor, money that Robert had been saving to cover some of the costs of the unfinished period of his apprenticeship. And there was a letter too — a letter thanking Master Allen for all his patience, help and the expertise of the training he had provided, with an abject apology for breaking his contract and leaving without permission.

The family met round the breakfast table, but each seemed subdued and upset. Bernard noticed that Emma looked red-eyed. Had she been crying, and did she know something that he did not? Many apprentices terminated their own contracts early, but few would leave money to cover their expenses, as Robert had done. So Bernard could only sigh deeply. This was all highly annoying and inconvenient. Now he would have to seek another apprentice until he was able to initiate his own boys, Timothy and Thomas, into the trade.

When Emma discovered the neatly folded note in her pocket, she guarded her secret carefully. Only she knew that Robert was aiming for France in an attempt to find Hugh Wilmot. Working in the printing trade, he had learned from the news-sheets he had printed of the dramatic flight of the executed king's son, who had been crowned Charles II in Scotland on New Year's Day 1651. After his disastrous defeat by Oliver Cromwell and the New Model Army at the Battle of Worcester in September of that year, Charles had evaded capture by escaping in disguise to France. And it was none other than Henry Wilmot, Hugh's uncle, who had engineered his getaway. In all likelihood Hugh had accompanied him. Even though Robert knew that his chances of seeing Hugh were remote, for Henry Wilmot had recently been created Earl of Rochester, the strength of his longing to find his friend made him hopeful. If he failed, so Robert had told Emma, he planned to return to Taunton to set up his own printing business — and, he added wistfully, if Emma ever wished to find him, he would always be waiting for her there.

Aiming for Dover, Robert had a long, slow journey ahead of him. With little idea of the distance he must cover, or even of the way, he could only take his bearings from the sun, heading in a south-easterly direction. For a day or two he walked briskly, sometimes begging a lift from a farmer as his wagon rumbled past along the narrow dirt tracks that crisscrossed the countryside. Before long Robert's small supply of bread and cheese was exhausted and he was obliged to buy what provisions he could from market stalls along the way. As night fell he would search for a barn, or even a hedgerow, where he could sleep, fearing the cost of the wayside inns and also the risk that someone might report the runaway apprentice to a local magistrate.

Robert had been on the road for four days. Dusty, unshaven and weary, he lay down in what appeared to be a deserted barn and within a moment or two was fast asleep. He did not hear footsteps approaching the barn or wake when hands began to grope under his cloak, searching for any money he might be carrying. With one deft stroke of a knife the string round his waist was cut and his purse, containing all his remaining money, was in the hands of thieves who had been tracking him for the last hour. Not until he was back on the road the following morning did Robert discover his loss. A wave of utter desolation swept over him. Alone, penniless, hungry and lost, he sat down and wept — tears of self-pity and despair.

He must return to the barn. It might be that his purse was still there — that seemed his only hope. Forlornly Robert searched among the bales of hay where he had been lying but could find nothing. Suddenly he froze: footsteps! He remained absolutely still; then in the dim half-light he saw a middle-aged woman, probably the farmer's wife, entering the barn. She had come to collect a bale of hay, and quickly spotted Robert. With a suppressed scream she turned to run, but then something about the young man made her hesitate. Was it his frightened face, his despondent look? She could not be sure. 'What do you think you are doing here?' she demanded.

'I am looking for my purse,' Robert replied steadily, 'but I fear it is stolen.' By this time the two had emerged into the full morning light. Carefully the farmer's wife scrutinized his face. 'I think I have seen you before...' she began slowly. Robert looked startled. Should he make a bolt for it? But he stayed. 'I believe you used to sit at the back of our meeting house in Great St Helen's and listen to Master

Knollys,' continued the woman. 'Weren't you Master Bernard Allen's apprentice?' No way of escape seemed open, and Robert had little alternative but to admit the truth.

'I was, madam, but now I have finished my apprenticeship. I am wishing to go to Dover and then to France, but have been robbed of all my savings.'

Throwing her plump arms in the air, Joan Lambert, for that was her name, exclaimed, 'Dover, young man! Why, you are not even at Rochester! You must come to the farmhouse along the lane, wash yourself and have some breakfast.'

Grateful in spite of his fears, Robert followed the woman along a muddy track until the farmhouse came in view, nestling in a small hollow among the trees.

A large, red-faced man greeted his wife in surprise. 'An extra farmhand?' he asked jovially.

'I think not,' she replied tersely.

Robert recognized him instantly. This was the very man he had once hidden behind to escape Hanserd Knollys' piercing gaze in the meeting house.

After a generous farm breakfast of rye bread, bacon and a large mug of ale, Robert shouldered his bag once more, but as he turned to go he felt a strong grasp on his arm. 'Stop!' commanded Harry Lambert. 'I hear you have been robbed; you must tell me more.' Gradually the whole story came out: of James, of Hugh Wilmot, his hopes, his plans, and even of the money he had left behind to terminate his apprenticeship. When Harry Lambert learned that Robert was a farmer's son, he had a suggestion: 'You are just the man I need here at Dale Farm for a few weeks while I harvest the hay. Stay until you have earned enough money to pay for your travel back to your home or to wherever you wish to go. But I fear your hopes of finding Master Hugh Wilmot are small indeed. I hear his uncle, the Earl of Rochester, travels widely in the service of Charles, son of our executed king. One thing I do insist is that you send a message to your father telling of your present circumstances and where you are.'

Thankful for such a suggestion, Robert agreed and even began to recognize that, despite everything, God had not forgotten him and perhaps behind all his troubled circumstances there was some divine plan for his life being worked out.

8.
THE CALL OF HOME

When a message arrived at Moorside Farm bringing the news of Robert's whereabouts, Alice wept with relief. After hearing from Master Bernard Allen of her son's unaccountable disappearance, her distress had been acute. How well she knew his determination, his impetuosity! She guessed that he might have hatched some hare-brained idea of finding Hugh Wilmot, but when she heard that he was safe and with friends she felt an overwhelming gratitude to God for his pity and kindness.

Now feeling the pressure of the years, Alice and Nicholas often wondered how long they could maintain the farm. Their old friend Walter Bayes was crippled with arthritis, and his gnarled, crooked fingers could no longer grip the shears or grapple with an unruly animal. But he still did what he could, and his presence in their home had been a comfort and support. Often he listened quietly as Alice and Nicholas discussed their problems, only venturing an opinion when he was asked. On many occasions his advice, springing from his deep knowledge of the Scriptures and his love of the Saviour, proved to be right. Alice knew that he prayed daily for Robert even though he had never met the youth, and he was confident that one day his prayers for his kind benefactors' only surviving son would be answered. Now in need of an extra farmhand, Nicholas often thought wistfully of Robert and wished he might come home and shoulder some of the responsibility. Meanwhile he decided to employ another village boy to come in each day and undertake some of the responsibilities on the farm.

The small thatched meeting house hidden in the dense forest on the edge of West Sedge Moor was crowded each week with men, women and young people, Although the laws demanding attendance only at parish churches had been eased, their pastor, Francis Bartlett, was still wary. He knew only too well that at any moment the political climate could change, and that angry Royalist politicians and bigoted churchmen alike were waiting to reimpose harsh and repressive laws on the Independent churches.

Meanwhile Robert repaid the generosity of farmer Harry Lambert and his wife by working hard on the farm — a thing he had never troubled to do at home. In response the tall, genial farmer and his warm-hearted wife cared for Robert like a son. They had often longed for a family of their own and lavished on Robert a warmth of affection he had missed since he had left home over five years ago. His relationship with Bernard and Sarah Allen had been formal at best, and their clear disapproval of any affection between the apprentice boy and their daughter Emma had bred a deep-seated resentment in Robert's mind.

Dale Farm

Even though haymaking had long finished, Robert reluctantly realized that even if he managed to find Hugh, the chances of speaking to him were remote. Instead he decided to stay on at Dale Farm for a while. Perhaps he might be able to accumulate enough money to set up his own printing business in Taunton, as he had promised Emma that he would.

In common with his own parents and with Bernard and Sarah Allen, the Lamberts refused to worship at the local parish church, choosing instead to travel each Sunday to nearby Rochester and join with a growing number of Baptists who, like their previous pastor Hanserd Knollys, believed strongly that a true church consisted only of those whose lives demonstrated a living faith in Jesus Christ and who had a desire to live in a way that was pleasing to God.

Robert still found it hard to comprehend such principles. Instead of accompanying his new friends to Rochester on

Sundays he was free to please himself on that day. Sometimes he went for long walks in the Kent countryside; at
other times he browsed among the books he discovered on
a small shelf in the family living room, hoping he might
find some tale of adventure in which he could immerse
himself. But they all seemed to consist of sermons, and
more sermons. On one wet Sunday as the rain sheeted
down outside, Robert had little alternative but to pick up
one dusty volume.

   He opened it casually. With a printer's eye he looked at
the font, then at the elaborate wood carvings of the decora-
tive initial letters with which each chapter began. Perhaps
some apprentice just like himself had toiled over those
letters, carving them out with painstaking care. It had been
printed some twenty years ago, and Robert found himself
wondering where that young man was now. Had he set up
a printing business of his own?

   This book was by someone with whom he shared a
name — a certain Robert Bolton — and it had a strange
title, *Comforting Afflicted Consciences*. As he glanced at the
first chapter, Robert found his interest stirred. It began by
quoting a verse from the Bible that he had never heard
before, one which ended with the question: '… a wounded
spirit who can bear?[1] Yes, he, Robert Wilkes, felt he had a
'wounded spirit', especially as he thought of the loss of his
only brother, of the disappointment he must be to his
parents, of the way he had cut short his apprenticeship,
and of Emma. But curing 'wounded spirits' — how was
that possible? Robert could think of no remedy apart from
forgetting the turmoil of former years and earning plenty
of money. Then perhaps he could make amends to his

ageing parents for his inconsiderate conduct and even provide a future and a home for Emma.

Glancing through the contents sheet at the front of the book, Robert noticed one section with the heading, 'The right method of curing an afflicted conscience'. Perhaps there would be some answers here. Turning the crisp pages carefully, some of which were still uncut, Robert found the place and scanned the text quickly.

Suddenly one sentence seemed to leap out at him, almost as though it had a life of its own:

> No sin of so deep a dye but Christ's precious blood can raze it out. No heart so dark and heavy, but one beam shining from his face can fill it as full of spiritual glory and joy as the sun is full of light.

Certainly he had heard that sort of truth before. He remembered Hanserd Knollys had said something similar about Christ being the 'only thing necessary'. But now, as he sat in a small, dimly lit farm living room with the rain sheeting down outside, Robert began to understand. A gleam of hope shone into his mind and a longing that one day he would fully grasp the truth conveyed by those words.

All of a sudden Robert heard a rattle in the yard as a small horse-drawn wagon drew up. Farmer Harry and his wife Joan had returned from the service they had attended in Rochester. Hastily replacing the book, and promising himself that he would read it more carefully another day, Robert sat down quickly, put his feet up on a stool and pretended that he had been asleep.

But he never did reread those words from Master Robert Bolton's treatise on afflicted consciences because the very next day a messenger boy cantered up the farm track raising clouds of dust as he came. He had an urgent summons for Robert from his father, Nicholas. He must come home immediately, for his mother was seriously ill and had been repeatedly calling for him. Robert had been with the Lamberts almost a year and to leave them was a painful wrench. But his mother in her weakness was asking for him. He must return to Somerset with all speed.

Borrowing a horse from Harry Lambert, Robert set off early the following morning. Most of his possessions he left behind, promising to return when he could. Urging the elderly mare onwards with all the speed her old legs could manage, Robert rode hard through Staines, Reading, Newbury, then through Trowbridge, Frome and south to the outskirts of Taunton. Overwhelmed with emotion as he rode though the familiar woods and the often-flooded meadows of his boyhood days, he pulled up just short of his home. He had left soon after his sixteenth birthday and now, in the spring of 1654, he was almost twenty-three. How could he ride along the very path where James had been mown down? Would he find his mother still alive? Almost unable to face going on, he suddenly saw someone coming towards him. Eyes blurred with tears, Robert scarcely recognized the man. Only when the figure broke into a run did he realize it was his own father, Nicholas. But, oh how changed! Now grey-haired and slightly stooped, he merely held out arms to welcome his homecoming son.

At first not a word passed between them. After a while Robert managed to say, 'Is she still alive?'

'Yes,' replied Nicholas, 'but only just. Maybe seeing you… Who knows?'

An air of desolation hung over the room where Alice lay, sleeping lightly, her hair, now grey, spread across the pillow. Her face was flushed with fever and on her hands and arms an ugly rash had broken out. Old Walter Bayes sat beside her bed, head in hands, but when Robert entered he looked up, smiled and rose to go. It would be an intrusion to stay.

Crossing over to the bed, Robert took his mother's hands in his — he could feel her burning fever — and at that moment she woke. Unable to speak much, she just whispered, 'You've come,' and held her son as if she could not let him go again. 'I prayed you would,' she murmured. That was all.

9.
TO PRINT ... OR NOT TO PRINT?

A loud knock at the farm door made them all jump. Alice had closed her eyes once more and seemed scarcely conscious. Robert was sitting beside his mother, silently praying — a thing he had rarely done before. With guilt and sorrow chasing each other through his mind, he could only beg that somehow she would recover. But the outlook was grave. An epidemic of typhus fever had broken out in the community. Alice had been visiting a sick friend who lived alone when only days later she too was taken ill. Her friend had subsequently died, and Nicholas held out little hope for his wife.

Surprised to have a visitor, Nicholas opened the door. There in the yard, still tethering his horse, was the town physician, Samuel Atkins. 'I hear your wife is ill,' he said abruptly. 'I have brought medication which I see as her only chance, for this epidemic has proved fatal in most cases.'

'But w...we didn't send for you, for we can scarcely p...pay for your good services, sir,' stammered Nicholas.

'I remember well your goodness to that young Wilmot boy, and wish to help you if that proves possible — but without charge,' replied the physician unemotionally.

Overwhelmed by such kindness, Nicholas could only shake Samuel Atkins' hand, his own tired features speaking his relief and gratitude as he led him to Alice's bedside.

But for Robert, if an angel had suddenly appeared from heaven in answer to his prayer, he could not have been more astonished than when Atkins arrived so unexpectedly. 'I have neglected God, and blamed him for the sorrows of my life,' thought Robert as he reproachfully looked back on his past. Yet in his pity God had answered his prayer in a moment, sending the town physician to his mother's bedside. And gradually, very gradually, as she sipped the bitter-tasting medicine day by day, Alice began to improve. First her temperature started to drop; then, as she was able, she accepted a little nourishment.

Two weeks later, still very weak, Alice was well enough to sit in the living room in the early spring sunshine; the rash was fading and the hacking dry cough a little easier. Meanwhile Robert attempted to busy himself in the kitchen — a new experience for him, but helped when possible by Walter. At first he resented the old man's presence in his home, but as the days passed he could hardly fail to notice the affection that shone in Walter's eyes both for his parents and now for himself. He began to regard him as the grandfather he had never known and before long found himself, hesitantly at first, chatting to the elderly man, then sharing some of the concerns that weighed on his mind, and even telling him about Emma.

At last Alice was well enough to resume her work, and Robert, a more considerate young man than he had been before, began to think about his own future. First he must return to his friends near Rochester to thank them once again for their kindness and to collect his belongings. With the money he had been saving it would be a good time to set up a printing business, and perhaps even to earn enough money to support his parents in their old age. But what about Hugh Wilmot? Although Robert had almost given up hope of ever seeing him again, he often wondered about him. Perhaps one day it might be possible... And then there was Emma. Unable to communicate with her over the past year, he could only imagine that so lovely a girl had either married someone else or had given up all hope of ever hearing from Robert again.

A measure of peace had now been restored in the country after the fearful bloodshed, anger and pain of the Civil War. Oliver Cromwell had recently taken firmer hold of power in the country by declaring himself Lord Protector. It seemed to Robert an ideal time for beginning his new enterprise in Taunton.

'I know of just the place for you to start,' ventured Nicholas. 'My friend Jack Peters has been looking out for a tenant for many months for the old lodge in Castle Street.'

Robert's heart sank as he viewed the semi-derelict property, once a lodge for visitors to Taunton Castle. Situated under the shadow of the grim turrets, its thick, whitewashed walls were flaking badly and the stone floor was sunken and irregular. But it was cheap and strategically placed, within easy reach of the town centre. 'I think I could use it, Papa,' said Robert, although he felt far from certain. Putting down a deposit, he began to lay plans for improving the old lodge and for buying his first printing press, inks, paper, and all that he would need.

Turret of Taunton Castle

He must also think of a name for his infant project, one that would interest and attract potential customers. Before long he was nailing a brand-new notice to the door:

Robert Wilkes
Printer
At the Sign of the Castle Gatehouse

Under the words was a logo depicting a menacing prison gate. But Robert well knew that there were also problems in the way of such an undertaking. Strict licensing acts had been reintroduced after the chaos of the Civil War, years during which literature of all sorts had poured from the presses: pamphlets, tracts, books, extolling every shade of political and religious opinion. Now anxious to suppress all Royalist propaganda that might militate against the newly established Commonwealth, the Rump Parliament had issued laws stipulating that no book could be printed without a licence. Censorship was rigorous. Anything thought to be in anyway controversial or not strictly favourable to present government policies was banned, while violations of such laws could bring heavy penalties, and even imprisonment. Robert would have to be very careful.

Restrictions on printers like Bernard Allen, working in the heart of London, were far more stringent than for those in country areas. Although no great problems existed as yet for Allen himself, as his views were largely in sympathy with the new Protectorate, any printer found producing material that was deemed questionable was first warned and then forced to close down his premises. Many

Castle Walk, Taunton

even took the precaution of removing their presses to some secret garret away from the ever-watchful eyes of government inspectors and informers.

Robert's small printing press gradually began to attract custom. Satisfied at the careful standard and speed at which the young man worked, a growing number of customers made their way to the press in Castle Street. At first small pamphlets appeared, and then larger works, each bearing the words, 'Printed at the Sign of the Castle Gatehouse', on the title page.

With business starting to prosper and his financial position more secure, Robert grew increasingly venture-some. Gone were the serious thoughts that had filled his mind as he had prayed at his mother's bedside; gone too was the nagging of a troubled conscience as he recalled the words of the preachers so favoured by his parents and friends. Instead the sound of that terrible groan from the crowd when Charles I was executed kept reverberating in his ears. 'How dreadful to kill the king!' he reflected angrily — and then he thought of Hugh. That fleeting glimpse of his scarred face among the crowd that day flashed before his eyes. Knowing little of the issues that had led to the king's execution, Robert became more daring in the sort of material he was prepared to print. Oh, yes, it was a risk, but perhaps he would escape being tracked down by the men paid by the Commonwealth government to check all printed matter.

Although Taunton had largely sided with Parliament during the war, many a disgruntled and resentful Royalist lived in the country areas surrounding Taunton. Often they nursed bitter sorrows over the death of fathers, brothers and sons, and antagonism was always simmering below the surface. When rumours began to circulate of a new printer who could be persuaded, possibly with a little financial inducement, to accept Royalist propaganda, Robert was assured of a steady supply of business.

Then one morning early in the summer of 1656 Nelly Smeaton appeared unexpectedly at the Sign of the Castle Gatehouse. Robert was startled and instantly captivated.

He had heard of Earl and Lady Smeaton's dashingly beautiful young daughter and somehow guessed that this tall, black-haired girl, elegantly dressed, with a sweet persuasive voice and dark eyes that seemed to roam restlessly back and forth, was indeed the girl that everyone admired. The earl and his wife lived in a cottage within sight of the ruins of their old manor house, destroyed in the violent clashes between Roundheads and Cavaliers during the war. Soon after Nelly's birth her older brother Jackie, still only sixteen, had enlisted in the Royalist army but had been killed at the Battle of Langport — the very conflict that had led to the death of Robert's only brother, James, and to Hugh Wilmot's disfiguring wounds.

Nelly was carrying a manuscript which her father wanted Robert to print, and in her hand was a packet containing a generous sum of money. Robert felt a swift uneasy pang. He well knew how bitterly angry Lady Smeaton still felt over the death of her only son, but how could he refuse this alluringly attractive girl, as she tossed her long dark hair and smiled so charmingly? Helplessly he held out his hand and took the manuscript. One quick glance told him that it was dangerously provocative material, its anti-Protectorate invective decidedly risky. With a high-pitched laugh, Nelly made a graceful exit, leaving Robert with a dilemma of major proportions.

Thoughts of his parents, of the kindness of the Lamberts in Rochester, of Francis Bartlett, to whose preaching he had listened as a boy, flashed through his mind. He remembered God's swift answer to his prayer for his mother. All seemed to be warning him with one voice against printing the vitriolic material in his hand, named appropriately enough, *The Freeman Chronicles*. Then he thought of Hugh and of the execution of the king. Impetuous and daring by nature, he made his decision. Yes, he would print it, and only hope that it would not come to the attention of the Licensing Office. With Nelly's ringing laugh still sounding in his ears, Robert began to set up the print and by the time the young woman returned three days later he had the proofs ready.

And so *The Freeman Chronicles* were printed. Now circulating freely, the pamphlet had apparently passed unnoticed by the censors. After several months Robert began to breathe more freely — until one morning in July 1656. He arrived at the press from his cottage on the outskirts of Taunton, and to his dismay saw at once that the door had been forced open. Thieves! It must be thieves! Hurrying inside, he could scarcely believe the devastation that met his gaze. His elegant printing press had been smashed to pieces; splinters of wood lay scattered everywhere. Inks had been poured out, papers ripped up.

He was finished — all was over with his venture into printing. Clearly the inflammatory pro-Royalist *Freeman Chronicles* had indeed come to the attention of the local licensing officers. For a full hour Robert sat on a small three-legged stool, the only item of furniture still intact, stunned. Then he realized he was in imminent danger. At any moment local magistrates could arrive to arrest him. With nothing worth salvaging, Robert could only be grateful that he had not left his takings at the press, or he would be destitute indeed. He must gather together his few possessions and leave Taunton as quickly as possible

Dismay was written on Alice's features as Robert arrived at Moorside Farm with his sorry tale. Both she and Nicholas knew that it would only be a matter of time before the magistrates tracked down their son. Then who could tell what the consequences might be, not just for his future, but for theirs too? As magistrates only had authority within the borders of their own county, it was imperative that Robert should leave Somerset immediately. 'You must not stay, my son,' urged Nicholas, 'no, not a day. Go to your friends near Rochester until I send word that it is safe to return.'

'My young friend,' called a frail old voice from the back bedroom. Walter Bayes was far from well. Although he was never one to admit to his weakness, it had been clear for some months that he was failing fast. Now he was bedridden and grieving constantly at the burden he was placing on Alice, who had never been strong since her serious illness. Robert answered the call and found old Walter propped up in his bed. With his dim blue eyes fixed on Robert, he urged him in a hoarse whisper: 'Go to London, my boy, go to London first and see if you can find that girl you love.' Robert stared back in surprise. How could this dying man be thinking about his concerns and longings?

'And never forget,' continued Walter, bringing out the words with difficulty, 'never forget those words that say, "Hope in the LORD: for with the LORD there is mercy…"'[1] Bending over, Robert strained to catch the old man's next words: 'I have fallen many times in my life … but the Lord has never let me go.' Like a shaft of light penetrating the gloom of his predicament, Walter's words brought a momentary ray of hope as Robert turned quickly to leave.

10.
THE END OF AN ERA

'Impossible!' thought Robert. How could he find Emma in a time of disgrace such as this? In his dreams he had imagined making a name for himself, of becoming wealthy and influential, and then one day claiming the girl for himself as he rode on a wave of popularity. Now he despised himself for such foolish fantasies. In the light of cold reality, he well knew that Emma might already be married. And in any case her parents would never agree to her marrying a former apprentice boy. All the same, some inner impulse urged him to ride through London on his way to Rochester. How easily he could have travelled through Reigate and Croydon, but somehow he found himself heading towards Slough, then Richmond and on through the old city.

Ever wary in case copies of *The Freeman Chronicles* had somehow been circulating as far as London, Robert rode mainly at night. Bishop's Gate Street seemed strangely deserted as he passed along it late one evening. Into

Threadneedle Street he rode, to allow himself a brief glimpse down Old Broad Street. There he could see the board advertising 'The Sign of the Morning Star' shimmering in the light of a full moon. He thought of that place where he had toiled for so long as an apprentice. Even now Emma might still be living there. Then he dared to raise his eyes a little higher and look at the window immediately below his own old attic room — her room. He almost choked with excitement for, silhouetted by the flickering candlelight, he was sure he caught sight of the shadowy figure of a young woman. It must be Emma — it must! Perhaps she had not married after all. Then, drawing his cloak closer around him, just in case anyone should recognize him, Robert urged his horse onwards — he dared stay no longer.

When Robert cantered at last up the well-known track leading to Dale Farm, Joan Lambert was in the yard feeding the chickens. At the sight of Robert she threw her plump arms up in the air in astonishment, just as she had done when she first discovered him in the barn. Then, quite as suddenly, she drew her apron over her kindly face and began to sob. Hastily dismounting, Robert stood irresolute and embarrassed on the path. At last Joan regained control, and Robert learned with consternation that Farmer Harry had recently fallen from the top of a rickety ladder in the hay-barn and had damaged his back. How seriously he was injured, Joan did not know, but the physician had ordered complete rest for at least three months — a critical situation for the farm. 'And I prayed you would come, I did; and here you are!' she finished with a sniff.

Robert shifted his feet sheepishly. What could he say? But in his heart he suddenly felt an unexpected surge of joy. He was needed, in spite of all his waywardness — here were kind friends who still wanted him and to whom he might even repay some debt of kindness.

'As long as you need me I will stay,' he reassured the distressed woman, and followed her into the dimly lit kitchen where Harry was lying on the old couch, clearly in some pain. Harry listened in silence to Robert's story. He made no comment, merely nodded and told Robert that his arrival was a remarkable provision for their need — without such help Harry might have to sell the farm, for neither Joan nor any of the farmhands he employed could manage alone.

Within hours Robert was back at work; soon the change and bracing outdoor life revived his spirits, and the gratitude Farmer Harry and his wife expressed lifted the cloud of despair. Slowly regaining strength, Harry began to hobble around the farm, helping where he could.

When Robert received news from home not many weeks later telling him that his old friend Walter Bayes had died, he was grieved but not surprised. Again and again Walter's last words rang in Robert's ears: 'Hope in the LORD: for with the LORD there is mercy.' 'Perhaps,' thought Robert, 'God may yet have mercy even on me.' But when he heard that Walter had eventually managed to sell his cottage after the rough mercenary soldiers had vacated it, and had left half of the money to him and the other half to his parents, his sense of unworthiness, coupled with gratitude, was almost overwhelming.

Long after Farmer Harry had fully recovered, Robert stayed on at Dale Farm. But he was becoming restless and

Oliver Cromwell

lonely. Kind though the Lamberts were, he knew he could not stay much longer. Then came astonishing news. The sultry summer days of 1658 had given way to violent thunderstorms, but on 30 August a storm broke over London so fearful in its proportions that even as far off as Rochester the thunder reverberated and the lightning tore the skies in two. Oliver Cromwell, Lord Protector of England, lay dying. Four days later he was dead! Perhaps, suggested Harry, that storm might have been a prediction that troubled days were lying ahead for England. The strong man at the helm of government since the fearful slaughter and chaos of the Civil War had succumbed to a fever, and was gone — it was the end of an era. And in his last moments, so Robert learned, this rugged soldier-statesman was still praying for the people over whom he ruled. This threw a new light on Cromwell as far as Robert was concerned. Until now all the young man could think about had been the groan uttered by the people as Charles I was executed. Perhaps there was another side to the story.

Cromwell's death was a decisive moment for Robert. He knew he must return to Somerset. As gently as he could, he broke the news to his friends Harry and Joan: 'I feel the time has come for me to go home. With so much political uncertainty, my unwise act will now be forgotten, and my parents need me now that old Walter's gone.'

'Well, my boy,' boomed the genial farmer, his face even redder than usual, 'we shall miss you sorely, but my good wife here and I have also decided we must soon sell Dale Farm and move back to London. These are uncertain days, and who can tell how long we may be able to worship our God in peace? We feel we shall be safer in London and, besides, my back has not been the same since my fall.'

'I will never forget your kindness,' said Robert with sincerity as he prepared to leave a few days later. 'And may the God you trust protect and keep you.' The words came out in a rush as Robert blushed crimson.

'And I too have a word for you, my young friend,' retorted Farmer Harry, 'a word that has carried me all my long days, through my many sins and failures.' Robert held his breath, for he had already guessed what the next words might be: 'Hope in the Lord, Robert, "Hope in the LORD: for with the LORD there is mercy..."' And with those very same words spoken earlier by old Walter ringing in his ears, Robert rode off into the distance, bound for Langport and home.

11.
A LETTER FROM EMMA

The year was 1660. Two years had passed since the death of Oliver Cromwell — years of anarchy and confusion in the land. Fearing that civil war might break out again, nobles and many churchmen had joined in extending an invitation to Prince Charles, eldest son of the executed king, to return from exile and take his father's throne. Now the nation had gone mad with joy and anticipation. At last the country would have a king once more; peace, tolerance and prosperity would prevail.

'Try not to worry, Alice,' said Nicholas tenderly to his wife. 'Our new king has promised us liberty of conscience. You may be sure he will keep his word.' But Alice was not convinced.

'You have always feared the worst,' continued Nicholas. 'All will be well, and no one will disturb our worship, nor will anyone stop Mr Francis from preaching the true word of God, as he has done these last fifteen years.'

Robert remained strangely silent as his parents were discussing the situation. Usually full of strong and often controversial opinions, he was rarely slow to add his views. But that day he said little. Now almost twenty-eight, he had remained single and seemed unaccountably indifferent to the various young ladies introduced to him by his parents and friends. Occasionally he accompanied Nicholas and Alice to Red Hill Meeting House, the chapel hidden in the woods above West Sedge Field Moor. More often he spent his time on a Sunday walking across the moors, or perhaps reading some political reports, or even carving small objects out of wood — a skill for which he revealed an unusual gift.

But on the last few Sundays he had saddled his horse and ridden off without saying a word. Nor did he make any comment on his activities when he returned as night was falling. Yet Alice could tell that her son was worried. If only he would speak to her!

In fact Robert had been mingling among the crowds of men and women attending St Mary Magdalen Church in Taunton. The handsome church tower, steeped in history, soared high in the air, dominating the town. But it was not the magnificent tower, nor the beauty of the building, established more than three hundred years before, that attracted Robert. A few weeks earlier he had received a letter — a letter from none other than Emma. She spoke of his friends, Harry and Joan Lambert, who had recently returned to London after selling their farm in Rochester. Now living in a small house in Lombard Street, they had paid a visit to Bernard and Sarah Allen. Knowing something of the friendship between Emma, who was now nearly twenty-four, and Robert, they had secretly given her

St Mary's Church, Taunton

details of his whereabouts and told her of all that he had meant to them. And it was Emma who had written to Robert persuading him to attend St Mary's.

Apparently, so Emma told him, a young preacher named Joseph Alleine had become the assistant minister there, and his lively preaching was attracting vast crowds. Would Robert go and hear him for her sake, if for no other reason? Robert read and reread the letter until the page was worn and tattered, and did exactly as she asked. Right at the bottom of the page, however, was one vital sentence. If it had been written in letters of gold, it could not have been of more value. Consisting of just four words, it read: 'I am still waiting.' It was all he had wished to hear.

How young the preacher looked! In fact Joseph Alleine was three years younger than Robert himself, yet his words riveted Robert's attention and scorched his conscience. Sometimes he plugged his fingers in his ears. He could scarcely bear to listen:

> O sinner, stop here and consider! If you are a man and not a senseless block, consider. Think where you are — standing upon the very brink of destruction. As the Lord lives, and as your soul lives, there is but a step between you and this. You do not know when you lie down, but you may be in hell before morning...

Oh, why did Emma wish him to hear such alarming words? Yet in his heart Robert knew they were true. Each night he tossed and turned on his bed. Accept them, he could not. But he could not reject them either. And the following Sunday it was the same. 'You are a lost man,' cried the preacher in a voice of full of pity, yet firm and challenging, 'if you hope to escape drowning on any other plank save Jesus Christ.'

'I will never go again,' thought Robert. But next Sunday he was back, hidden in a corner behind one of the massive fluted pillars. Sunday after Sunday it was the same. Sometimes he felt that God might yet have mercy on him. Then he would find himself floundering in despair — until at last one Sunday he heard words that seemed to search him out, hidden as he was behind a huge pillar. 'Oh, the kindness of God, his boundless compassion, his tender mercies!' cried the preacher. 'Has he not said to you, poor man that you are, hiding in some corner, has he not said, "Hope in the LORD: for with the LORD there is mercy"? Yes, there is mercy even for you.'

How could Joseph Alleine possibly see him behind the pillar? How could he know that this was the very verse that old Walter Bayes and Farmer Harry had both quoted? Robert asked himself in astonishment. Who could have told him? But it was like an arrow that flew right to the mark. Yes, there was mercy even for him, and right there, hidden from the gaze of all around, Robert cried out to God for that mercy. He rode home that day with a light heart — the burden of years had lifted from his shoulders. With a mother's intuition, Alice knew even before Robert told her that her son had found the peace with God that had so long eluded him.

How Robert wished he could get in touch with Emma! If only he could write to her, but he feared any letter would be intercepted, and would only cause trouble for her. At last he made up his mind. He would spend some days in London and perhaps find a way to see her.

Bitter blizzards had swept across the country late in December 1660 and not until early in January 1661 did Robert venture to visit the capital once more. Hardly had he arrived before he found himself caught up in a frenzied crowd: yells rang through the air; swords flashed silver in the pale winter sun. Whatever was going on? The military were out in force, and civilians, lightly armed, were attacking as viciously as they could with throaty shouts of 'For King Jesus! For Jesus! Rally to his standard. Slay his enemies... King Jesus!' Men were falling, wounded, dead — soldiers and citizens alike. Hastily reining in his horse, Robert turned down a narrow alleyway and waited, breathless and alarmed.

He had often heard from Bernard Allen of the extreme ideas of the men known as the Fifth Monarchists, whose slogan had always been 'For King Jesus'. He had even wondered at times whether Allen himself was a secret sympathizer. He recollected Allen's strange remark after the execution of Charles I about King Jesus being the next rightful monarch. These men and women, followers of leaders like Thomas Venner, the preacher at Swan Alley Meeting House, believed that the fifth and final kingdom prophesied in the biblical book of Daniel — the one destined to rule the world — was to be the kingdom of Christ. They held that the overthrow of Charles I marked the end of the fourth and last earthly kingdom. Now Christ must bring in his eternal kingdom. The throne of England was his by divine right, and he would set up his rule, bringing in a millennium of justice and peace. So when Charles II was restored to the throne the Fifth Monarchists, led by Venner, issued a call to arms. They were prepared to install Christ's kingdom by force if need be. Robert knew of these things, but had never for a moment imagined that he would be caught in the middle of such an armed uprising.

Then all went quiet. The fighting seemed to have moved further away, and Robert ventured from his hiding place. Suddenly his horse reared up in alarm for there, lying right across his path, was a man wounded in the fighting. The remembrance of Hugh Wilmot flashed across Robert's mind. His own father had faced a similar situation. 'How can I help this man?' he wondered wildly, dismounting from his horse. Stooping down, he looked more closely at the injured figure. Then he gasped in astonishment. Bernard Allen himself was lying there, possibly dying. Trembling all over, Robert leaned against his horse for a moment. Then he knew he must help. With strong arms he lifted Allen as gently as he could and laid him across the animal's back. He must take him home with all speed, for who could tell whether the military might be back at any moment to collect or kill the wounded?

Darkness had fallen by the time Robert reached Old Broad Street carrying his sad burden. Bernard Allen had shown no sign of life during that long walk. Perhaps he would regain consciousness back in the warmth and comfort of his own home, thought Robert as he timidly knocked on the heavy door of the Sign of the Morning Star. He scarcely knew what to say.

When Sarah Allen came to the door, her face grey and pinched with anxiety, she did not even spare a glance at the horseman — perhaps he was a soldier; she neither knew nor cared — but her startled cry at the sight of Bernard lying apparently lifeless across a horse brought the rest of the family running to the door. With infinite care she and her twin sons, Thomas and Timothy, now strong young men, lifted Bernard down and carried him indoors. 'Oh, why did he go? Why, oh why, did he go?' moaned Sarah over and over again as she disappeared into the house. Only Emma remained at the door. With tears streaming down her face, she turned to look at the horse-man who had brought her father home. For one brief moment their eyes met. Then, flinging her arms around Robert, she wept uncontrollably.

'You must go in now. You must,' whispered Robert urgently, pushing her away as gently as he could. 'I found your father lying in the road after the fighting had moved away, but I fear he is badly injured.'

'I beg you to stay,' cried Emma between her sobs.

'I dare not,' Robert replied, 'but, oh, Emma! I wanted to tell you that I too now know the forgiveness of God I have been seeking so long. This is why I came to London — to see you if I could.'

Then turning his horse sharply, Robert sprang into the saddle and cantered away, before his resolution failed him. Perhaps, just perhaps, if his prompt action were to save Bernard's life he might yet win a place of respect in Sarah's heart. He even dared to hope that she might begin to consider him a worthy husband for the girl he had loved for so long.

12.
AN UNEXPECTED MEETING

23 April 1661 dawned clear and bright. Today Charles II
was to be crowned King of England. From the early hours
of the morning crowds had been flocking to the capital to
gain some vantage point along the route that England's
new king would take as he rode across London for his
coronation. At last the waiting was over. Charles, decked
in gorgeous coronation robes, had left the stern battlements
of the Tower of London to ride towards Westminster
Abbey. Behind him in colourful pageant followed the
nobility: dukes, earls and bishops, all in a glittering array
of jewelled garments sparkling in the spring sunshine.

And among them rode Hugh Wilmot, nephew of the late
Lord Henry Wilmot, side by side with his cousin John
Wilmot, who had inherited his father's title as the second
Earl of Rochester. Hugh had never seen anything like this
before, nor could he have imagined such a day of splendour
and celebration. As he passed through the cheering, jubilant
crowds, mounted on his richly ornamented horse, his mind

was filled with hope and expectation. At last his war-torn country would be at peace.

Ever since the Fifth Monarchist uprising four months earlier, as Hugh well knew, the jails had been packed with innocent men and women, cast into prison without pity because they refused to attend the parish churches. Perhaps the new king would grant religious tolerance, thought Hugh hopefully. Although he was at a loss to understand why religious people should be so stubborn about the buildings in which they worshipped, he could not quite erase from his mind the views and the strongly held convictions of men and women like Nicholas Wilkes and his wife Alice; nor could he forget their kindness to him.

Sixteen years had passed since Hugh had been flung from his horse after the Battle of Langport in 1645. Now in his early thirties, he often found himself thinking of the young man who had tried to save his life on that fateful day and had lost his own in the attempt. He thought of Robert, younger son of Nicholas and Alice. 'I wonder where he is now,' mused Hugh as he cantered along the cobbled route. 'If only I could repay that family in some way! I expect Robert will be a married man by now, a farmer perhaps, and will have quite forgotten me.'

The years had been hard for Hugh Wilmot. The pain and disfigurement of his injuries had driven him into a lonely world of self-despair. Always conscious of his scarred face, he made few friends, while his injured leg would not allow him to share the sporting activities of other young noblemen. He hated yet feared his uncle, Henry Wilmot, Earl of Rochester, but had no option other than to obey his orders. For much of the time he had

**Henry Wilmot
Earl of Rochester**

accompanied Henry as he travelled across Europe trying to raise support for the exiled Charles.

Then in 1656 Lord Henry Wilmot had been appointed to a position of high command in the Royalist forces that were centred in the Belgian town of Bruges. The title of First Colonel of the Grenadier Guards had been conferred on him, adding to his already distinguished standing. Certainly the title was grand enough, but to Henry Wilmot's disgust the state of the quarters in which his regiment was billeted was far from satisfactory. With overcrowded and unsanitary conditions, his men were falling sick and dying of dysentery and other infections at an alarming rate.

The only consolation for Hugh himself had been the love of a gentle Dutch girl, Samile de Vries, who was working as a maid in the barracks. Henry Wilmot had opposed the marriage, considering Samile an unsuitable match for Hugh. 'That girl speaks no English, and her family is poor,' he said disparagingly. Dependent on his uncle financially, Hugh could do nothing except wait. Then quite unexpectedly Henry himself succumbed to an infection and, after a short illness, died in Bruges early in

1657. Hugh shed no tears for his uncle and only a month later he married Samile.

News of the death of the Lord Protector Oliver Cromwell in September 1658 brought a further change for Hugh. Now he planned to return to England with Samile after their first baby, due early in 1659, was born. There he would purchase a home, financed by the legacy left him by his uncle. But once again Hugh faced a crushing sorrow. Shortly after her baby was born, Samile, who was far from strong, died of childbirth fever. Nor did her infant son survive her for long. Bereft, embittered and alone, Hugh knew he must return to England, leaving behind two fresh graves, those of his wife and child. With little purpose left in life, he decided to train as a barrister. During the summer of 1659 he entered himself at Gray's Inns of Court. Perhaps, he thought, with a mixture of misery and ambition, he might be able to rise in the legal profession and gain eminence in that field despite his physical defects.

Like Hugh, Robert too hoped that the coronation of England's new king would usher in an era of peace and tolerance. But he was less optimistic than Hugh, having already experienced something of the malice of the new government towards the Independent churches. Now regularly attending the meeting house in the woods with his parents, he had noticed the growing number of empty seats; some who were once prominent members seemed to be unaccountably missing each Sunday. Fear — that was the explanation. Robert was sure of it. However plausible their excuses for absence might be, they were clearly desperate to protect themselves and their families from any danger. For, since the Fifth Monarchist rebellion, the authorities were watching closely for any sign of trouble.

Even their pastor, Francis Bartlett, had been briefly arrested and questioned. No one was sure what the future might hold.

With Nicholas now turned sixty-five, Robert had taken charge of Moorside. A better businessman than his father, he had employed two young men from the village to oversee the day-to-day management of the farm, while, with the legacy bequeathed to him by old Walter Bayes, Robert had built premises attached to the farmhouse where he had set up another printing press. A far less pretentious notice than his former one hung on the farm gate, merely announcing the press as 'Ye Olde Moorside Printing Works'. It would not be wise even to attach his name in case some magistrate with a long memory might recall the *Freeman Chronicles* fiasco of six years earlier.

But for Robert the highlight of each week was a letter from Emma, often telling of her father's steady improvement and always of her continued affection. Then came news that Bernard had recovered sufficiently to return to work and join his twin sons in the running of the Sign of the Morning Star.

Eventually, one day early in 1662, Robert received a letter in another handwriting — one from Sarah Allen herself, with an invitation to visit the family. Bernard owed his life to Robert, and Sarah knew it. She wished to thank him in person, but more importantly she said that if her daughter was agreeable she would no longer oppose the marriage.

Overjoyed, the young man set off for London dressed as handsomely as his limited funds would allow. Swiftly galloping through the crisp snowbound countryside, Robert's heart sang for joy. At last, at long last, he was welcome back at the Sign of the Morning Star and, above all, could claim Emma for his own. Thirteen years had elapsed since he first saw Emma as a shy but curious child peering into the room while he waited for his father to decide the terms of his apprenticeship with Bernard.

With his mind preoccupied, Robert twice missed his way in the city, his horse slithering in the slushy melting snow. At last he found himself on familiar territory in Gray's Inn Road. Now he must only turn left into Holborn Road, on into Newgate Street, then along Cheapside, into Threadneedle Street. Soon he would be knocking at that well-known door. In his excitement Robert spared only a passing glance for the Gray's Inn students thronging the entrance to the imposing Inn of Courts. All were laughing and chatting. Just one young man clothed in a trainee barrister's black gown and small black cap was lagging behind the rest. He had a severe limp. Almost immediately Robert found himself pulling up sharply, for he had nearly ridden straight into the man. 'I apologise, good sir. I must take more care in future,' Robert called out lightly.

Spinning round quickly, the student looked up at the speaker. Only then, as he noticed the ugly scar down one cheek, did Robert realize it was none other than Hugh Wilmot, looking much older, to be sure, than when Robert had last seen him, almost seventeen years earlier, but still with that same strong yet gentle face. With a gasp of surprise, he could only stammer, as he leaped down from his horse, 'Hugh, Hugh, it's Robert!'

To his astonishment Hugh leaned weakly against Robert's horse, too overcome to speak. At last, recovering his poise, Hugh began to tell him the long story of all that had happened in his life since last they met.

Robert, for his part, spoke of his sincere but frustrated desires to find Hugh again, and went on to tell him of the happy purpose of his present mission.

Finally, with both men shivering with cold, they arranged to meet up again before Robert's return to Somerset. 'And I shall be looking forward to a wedding,' said Hugh with a mischievous smile lighting up his sad face.

13.
JOY AND TRAGEDY

Hugh Wilmot did attend Robert and Emma's wedding celebrations in July 1662, but it was a quiet occasion, for the days were troubled. Held in the meeting house where Bernard Allen and his family now worshipped, it was attended by only a handful of invited guests. Any service not conducted in a parish church was frowned upon by the new Cavalier Parliament formed under Charles II, and could easily be interrupted, or even stopped by a local magistrate.

With Emma dressed in a simple white gown, her dark hair tied back with a ribbon, and Robert at her side in his best homespun breeches and light brown doublet, it was a joyful occasion. And few more cheerful guests were there to witness the ceremony than Joan and Harry Lambert. Joan's round face beamed with delight while tears of happiness rolled down her cheeks, and Farmer Harry glowed with pride almost as if he had been the groom's own father.

Hugh looked much grander than the bridegroom, in his scarlet doublet and white silk breeches, but the unselfish pleasure that lit up the young nobleman's face as he shared the enjoyment of the day was something that Robert would never forget. To be able to see Nicholas and Alice once more and to express his gratitude for their kindness all those years ago fulfilled one of Hugh's long-held desires.

Yet, joyful as the occasion was, neither Robert, Emma, nor their parents could look forward to the future days with any measure of confidence. Only two months before the wedding Parliament had passed the Act of Uniformity, stipulating that anyone who held a position of ministry or of leadership in the churches must 'openly and publicly declare before the congregation' that he agreed with everything contained in the newly revised *Book of Common Prayer*.

Robert knew that men like Joseph Alleine of St Mary's in Taunton, whose searching preaching had changed his life, would never consent to such conditions; much had been introduced into the Prayer Book which was contrary to the teachings of the Bible. A deadline, 24 August — St Bartholomew's Day — had been set, and anyone who had failed to comply by that date would automatically be debarred from any further ministry within his church. Only four weeks remained before St Bartholomew's Day. If men like Joseph Alleine were to be thrown out of their churches, how could they maintain their own and their family's livelihoods? This was the question on everyone's mind. And if clerics of the national church were treated so severely, what would happen to Independents like themselves?

True to their worst fears, on Black Bartholomew's Day, as it came to be known, at least two thousand men of faith and principle lost everything: home, ministry and income. Some families became destitute. Joseph Alleine, who was now prohibited from entering that grand old pulpit at St Mary's, continued to preach in homes, village halls and even barns — wherever he could gather together men and women bold enough to hear him. 'How can our government act like this?' Emma asked Robert in bewilderment. Sensitive as ever, she found it hard to contemplate such sufferings and, like many others, feared what might happen next.

Alice had welcomed her new daughter-in-law into the home with open arms. Approaching sixty years of age, she was aware of her declining strength, and the task of providing meals for hungry farm workers as well as for her family was an increasing burden. Added to this she was becoming deaf, and even her sight was not as keen as once it was. Living fairly near the small thatched meeting house in the Red Hill woods, she undertook tasks that few others seemed willing to do. Each Monday Alice could be found cleaning and tidying up the small building ready for the following Sunday.

'Why must you do it, Mama?' enquired Robert. 'Are there no others who could help you?' Although Emma was willing enough, Alice stoutly refused her offer. 'It is little enough for me to do for my Saviour who has done so much for me,' was her constant reply. But Robert was not happy. Who could tell whether his mother might find herself in some danger in such a lonely spot? With no one within earshot to help if anything should happen, she could fall, or even be taken ill. So concerned did Robert

Loughwood Meeting House, in nearby Devon, is a typical Dissenting meeting house from the time of this story.

become, particularly in the gloomy December afternoons as 1662 drew to a close, that he made a habit of delivering proof sheets or specimen copies of his work to distant customers on a Monday afternoon and calling in briefly at the meeting house as he was returning home.

But on his approach to the wood one afternoon just as darkness was gathering, Robert was startled to see two men running out from between the trees. Then he saw a black curl of smoke hovering over the woods. Perhaps the men had lit a bonfire which was now out of control. 'But whoever could be lighting a fire at a time like this?' he wondered uneasily. As he entered the woods, the strong acrid smell of burning grew more intense. Even his horse seemed restive and unwilling to proceed. Then he saw it in the distance. The meeting house was alight. Terrified, he spurred his animal desperately onward. Fastening the reins quickly round a tree stump to secure the frightened horse, Robert rushed forward on foot towards the door, which his mother always left open when she was in the building. 'Mama! Mama!' he cried, but there was no answer. Quickly he tied his cravat around his nose and mouth and dashed into the burning building. Dimly through the smoke he could see his mother lying on her face, unconscious. Choking as the smoke and flames swirled above him, he grabbed her by her arms and dragged her through the open door.

At that very moment a strong gust of wind sent the flames roaring through the thatch, engulfing the little meeting house in their fiery embrace. Robert was only just in time. Gathering all his strength, he lifted the uncon-scious form in his arms and staggered forward, carrying her as gently as he could. Just as he reached the outskirts of the wood he heard the welcome sound of wagon wheels approaching. Nicholas had seen the smoke from the farmhouse window and had ridden hastily to investigate.

Not a word passed between father and son as they laid Alice in the wagon as carefully as they could, her dishevelled grey hair lying across her still face. Robert, his hands scorched by the flames, went back to fetch his horse. But it had broken loose and was nowhere to be seen. With bigger concerns on his mind, and knowing that the animal was probably already home by now, Robert strode off after his father.

Only when they reached the farm could they begin to see the extent of Alice's injuries by the spluttering light of the oil lamps. Emma bathed the burns on Alice's face and hands with tepid water and wrapped a blanket round her while Robert hurried out into the night to call the town physician Samuel Atkins. Forgetful of his own pain, his only concern was to save his mother if it was possible, however much it might cost. Atkins, who was in his nightshirt and sleeping cap by the time Robert arrived, grumbled good-naturedly, dressed again, gathered some ointment and some laudanum to act as an opiate and followed Robert into the night.

There was little Atkins could do by the poor light of the oil lamps, apart from covering Alice's burns with his own special ointment and then with soft cloths. Finally he treated Robert's painful hands, before promising to return. By morning Alice had regained consciousness, but could tell them little apart from the fact that she had heard two men outside the meeting house. She had decided it was best to ignore them and because of her deafness had failed to hear the first faint crackle of flames. Not until thick smoke was billowing around her did she realize the danger she was in. By then it was too late.

When Samuel Atkins returned the next day he confirmed what the family feared — that the meeting house had been burned down deliberately by men determined to stamp out the worship of Independent churches. And theirs was not the only one to be destroyed that night. At least two others in the area had been burned to the ground, but Alice had been the only casualty. Now they knew for certain what they had anticipated for months. From this time on they would only be able to worship in secret.

Then, with typical professional brevity, Samuel Atkins told them that the outlook for Alice was bleak at best. Severe shock, combined with her age, the intensity of her pain and the degree of her burns, gave her physician little hope of her recovery. All he could do was to alleviate her pain as much as possible.

Too stunned to react, the family could only sit around Alice's bed in dismayed silence.

14.
THE TWO ALICES

For three long days Nicholas had sat by his wife's bedside, scarcely eating, scarcely sleeping. Emma undertook all the household duties while Robert hovered anxiously around, trying to concentrate on his work, but finding himself far from able. Alice had spoken little during this time. Her pain was intense; at times she seemed to lose consciousness. 'Soon I shall be where pain and sorrow can never come,' she had murmured on the third evening after the burning of the meeting house, adding slowly, '… but for you … oh, Nicholas…!' Her words trailed off; then she appeared to be unconscious once more. It was the last she spoke: before dawn broke the next day Alice had left her poor suffering body behind.

The burial was a simple ceremony led by their pastor Francis Bartlett. Alice's grave was in the unconsecrated portion of the Langport parish graveyard, an area reserved for infidels and for any who described themselves as Nonconformists or Independents. Her loss was a bitter blow, and it seemed that Nicholas had aged many years overnight. He spoke little, but spent much of his time reading through portions of his worn old Bible, pages from the last book of the New Testament, the book of Revelation, becoming tearstained and torn. 'There shall be no more death, neither sorrow, nor crying...', Emma heard him repeating over and over. It seemed as if his spirit was already treading the threshold of that land which Alice had reached before him.

Only one thing lightened the sorrow of those days: Emma's first child was due in June. Disappointed though they were that Alice had not lived to see her grandchild, they well knew that her present joys were beyond the greatest this earth could offer. Added to this, an air of uncertainty and fear rested on all the members of the small Independent church. With their building reduced to ashes, the congregation now had nowhere to meet. To worship in any single place for long was certainly unsafe. Who could tell what might befall a family in whose house they decided to meet regularly? Everyone was on edge, especially as no one had been brought to justice for the crime that had led to Alice's death.

The Cavalier Parliament, which now ruled the country under Charles II, was bent on revenge for the defeat that had befallen the Royalists during the Civil War. Some had suffered the loss of property; others had been imprisoned, and many had lost sons, brothers and friends in battle. Not enough for them were the executions of prominent Commonwealth politicians and the degradation of Oliver Cromwell's body as retribution for the death of Charles I. Following the restoration of his son to the throne, Parliament's undisguised aim was a determination to stamp out

every residue of nonconformity in religion. Under the
guidance of the new archbishop, Gilbert Sheldon, the
government resolved to bring the nation to a uniform style
of worship, allowing no deviation from the High Church
stance reflected in the revised *Book of Common Prayer*.

The situation for former ministers of the established
church who were unable to consent to the terms of the new
Prayer Book was becoming increasingly tenuous. Joseph
Alleine, dismissed from his pulpit at St Mary's, Taunton, in
August 1662, had occasionally preached in the small
thatched meeting house hidden in the Red Hill woods. As
soon as he heard of the tragedy that had befallen the
Wilkes family he had been among the first to visit Nicholas, Robert and Emma. Unknown to Robert at the time,
Alleine had prayed earnestly for him when the young man
first started attending St Mary's. Few had expressed
greater joy than when he heard of Robert's new-found
faith.

Then in May 1663, just five months after Alice's death,
and only a few weeks before Emma's baby was due, came
further disturbing news: Alleine had finally been arrested
and confined to Ilchester Jail — a notorious, crowded and
filthy place.

'But what has he done?' asked Emma in dismay.

'Nothing, nothing at all,' replied Robert, 'except preach
wherever people were willing to hear.' The anger at such
fearful injustice welled up inside him as he thought of that
fine, other-worldly man cast into prison for no other reason
than that of fulfilling his calling as a preacher.

Rumour had it that Alleine was obliged to trudge the
twenty-five long miles from Taunton to Ilchester carrying
his own arrest warrant with him. But he did not go alone.

For some miles along the way the roads were lined with weeping men and women, grieving that so well-loved a preacher should be treated in such a disdainful fashion. When Alleine arrived the jailer was nowhere to be found. To the secret amusement of many who heard of it, Alleine, with astonishing boldness, took the oppor-

Joseph Alleine

tunity of gathering a crowd together and preaching for one last time at the prison gate before an embarrassed jailer arrived and hastily hustled him inside.

Not only had Alleine been imprisoned, but other preachers in the area had also been arrested and were being held in Ilchester Jail, awaiting trial by Sir Robert Foster at the Quarterly Assizes. Clearly the authorities were determined to crush all preaching outside the established churches. How long would their own pastor, Francis Bartlett, remain a free man, thought Robert nervously. And what about himself? With his father increasingly frail, Robert was now taking a more prominent part in the life of the church, and since the fire the congregation had sometimes met at Moorside Farm.

When Sarah Allen came down to Somerset early in June to be with her daughter during her confinement, Robert felt a measure of relief. With Emma under her mother's watchful eye, Robert decided to visit Alleine in jail. Saddling his horse, he set off one hot June day, the journey taking him the best part of four hours. But nothing prepared him for the situation he discovered when he reached Ilchester. Knocking loudly on the heavy door of the jailer's quarters, Robert gained permission to visit the prisoner. 'He's up there with all those other rogues,' said the jailer coarsely, pointing up the creaking stairway that led to the Bridewell Chamber — a name given to the room on the upper floor where petty criminals were incarcerated.

Robert gazed in bewilderment at the scene that met his eyes. Sixty or more men were crammed in together into that limited space, lying in rows on straw mats with scarcely any room to move. At least six other local preachers were there, some already known to Robert. One, John Norman, a highly respected preacher from Bridgwater whom Robert had met on several occasions, lay next to Alleine at the far end of the room. Together with these men, about fifty Quakers had been cast into prison on the same indictment — either caught preaching or listening to preaching.

The merciless June sunshine that beat down on the sloping prison roof had raised the temperature to an intolerable level. So low was the ceiling that Robert could not walk upright, but had to bend double, as he stepped carefully over the rows of pitiful prisoners until he reached Alleine. The atmosphere was stale and sultry, the odour pungent and vile. Vermin crept up the walls and massed together in every dark corner. A chorus of crude blasphemies and curses, together with the rattle of chains, could be heard wafting up from the prison cells below where villains of every shade were huddled together, many awaiting execution for their crimes.

And still more men, rounded up like common criminals, were being packed into the Bridewell Chamber, even while Robert was speaking to Mr Alleine. To his astonishment a look of quiet triumph rested on Alleine's features despite the streams of sweat that rolled down his cheeks. 'Robert, my kind friend, welcome, welcome!' said Alleine heartily, and then added above the hubbub of noise and complaint, '"All that will live godly in Christ Jesus shall suffer persecution."[1] Remember that, young man, and God will give you strength to endure the evil day.'

Robert nodded dumbly. He thought of Emma. Oh, how could he bear such a situation? How could he leave her alone, if he too should be apprehended, especially at such a time? But Alleine seemed to read his mind: 'The cross of Christ is your crown, Robert; the shame of Christ your glory. This is the way of the kingdom.' Overcome by emotion, Robert could only squeeze Alleine's hand. He did not stay long, for soon the jailer's voice boomed over the hubbub, ordering him to leave. Giving the imprisoned preacher some homemade cakes which Emma had sent, Robert made his way out of the prison, stepping gingerly over each prisoner as he went.

Reaching fresh air at last, Robert gulped deeply and turned to fetch his horse. Just at that moment he heard angry shouts: a knot of men were hustling yet another captive into prison. Looking up quickly, he was horrified to see the ginger head of none other than his own pastor, Francis Bartlett, being pushed in through the heavily grated prison gate. With a surge of fury Robert lunged towards the men. How dare they treat good men like this!

'No, Robert, no!' shouted Bartlett. 'Keep away! God is my protector, never fear.'

Only just escaping himself from the grasp of angry men, Robert leaped onto his horse and shot off towards Langport, his mind a turmoil of indignation and fear.

At last Robert reached the farm and saw his father coming out to meet him, his face wreathed in smiles — almost the first time Robert had seen the cloud of loss lift from the old man's face. Robert guessed immediately. 'Emma! Emma!' he yelled. 'Is she all right?'

'Go and see, my son,' replied Nicholas. But Robert had heard a sound well before he reached Emma's side: a high-pitched infant's wail. The midwife was still bustling around when Robert burst into the room and saw Emma sitting up in bed tenderly cradling a dark-haired, red-faced little bundle, as his mother-in-law perched on the bed beside her. Wrapping his arms around his wife and small daughter, Robert wept for joy and relief. It had been a day of conflicting emotions — horror, fear, anger, relief and joy. How would he ever forget 6 June 1663?

'Shall we call her Alice?' said Emma, as she gazed at the child, her dark eyes tired, but shining with devotion.

15
THE CONVENTICLE ACT

Many of the imprisoned preachers and Quakers were released during the weeks ahead, for the charges against them made by an over-enthusiastic soldiery could not be substantiated. As yet there was no law against Independent congregations meeting together for worship; nor were pastors and preachers banned from ministering to them, however much the authorities might frown on the practice. In the uncertain days following the Restoration all such gatherings were regarded as a potential conspiracy, every meeting a likely hotbed of political dissidents in the eyes of the government.

Even though the Wilkes' own pastor, Francis Bartlett, was freed under caution, there was no such release for Joseph Alleine or for John Norman of Bridgwater. Robert had shuddered when he learned that none other than Sir Robert Foster, recently appointed as Lord Chief Justice and well known as a bitter opponent of Nonconformist preachers, was to act as judge at the West Country Summer

Assizes to be held in Taunton. 'What hope do these good men have of a fair trial?' he thought gloomily. Although Alleine had only been preaching to a small group of people in his own home when he was arrested in May 1663, he had been accused of behaving 'riotously and seditiously ... to the great terror of the King's subjects'.

The trial was a mockery of justice, as many had feared, with both preachers returned indefinitely to Ilchester Jail. But Judge Foster had come face to face with two of the finest men in the country. 'Did you hear what John Norman said to the judge when he pronounced that biased sentence against him?' Robert asked his father the day after the assizes. ' "Sir, you must ere long appear before a greater Judge to give an account of your actions, and for your railing on me, the servant of that great Judge." Those were his very words. I would certainly tremble,' Robert added, 'if I were in his position.' And few were surprised when only a week or two later the callous judge suddenly collapsed and died as he rode around the circuit passing unwarranted and cruel sentences on Quakers and Nonconformist preachers alike.

As 1664 dawned, everyone hoped the pressure on Nonconformists and Independent churches might ease. But far from it. If the preachers had borne the heaviest burden of the Cavalier Parliament's fears and antipathy, it was now the turn of the congregations — men and women like Bernard and Sarah Allen, Joan and Harry Lambert and, of course Robert and Emma Wilkes, with Robert's father, Nicholas. To prevent any secret plot being hatched to overthrow the present government — and certainly there had been some — an act was passed known as the Conventicle Act. Harsh in its terms, it forbade any gathering of five or more people, in addition to an immediate family group, for religious purposes. Those caught at such a meeting would immediately incur a fine of five pounds — a prohibitive sum for most families. If the worshipper refused to pay, or could not afford to do so, three months' imprisonment was the alternative punishment. Should someone be caught at worship again, the penalties were doubled: six months in jail, or a fine of ten pounds. And for persistent 'offenders' the possibility of deportation for seven years loomed as an ultimate punishment.[1]

'What are we going to do?' asked Emma, in bewilderment. She was expecting a second child in the autumn, and little Alice was less than a year old. What would happen if Robert was thrown into prison? How could they ever pay such a fine? Anxiety was written in every line of her face.

In reply Robert flung his arms around his wife, and answered tenderly but steadily, 'We will continue doing exactly what we have been doing.' Yet he sounded more certain than he felt. 'We will go on worshipping in different homes, and if that is difficult there are many secret dells and clearings in the forests where we can meet.'

Emma did not reply. The result of such a courageous stand was clear enough.

With their meeting house burned down and their pastor Francis Bartlett under constant observation, the dangers of worshipping together faced by the Independent church were high. Sometimes Moorside Farm, with its isolated location, was chosen as the best option. But Robert noticed sadly that the numbers prepared to risk attending from week to week were declining steadily. And always the excuses were different: the weather was too cold; the children were poorly; the horse needed to be shod; the chimney had caught alight; visitors had called... But again the underlying reason was the same: fear.

With the approach of summer the congregation gathered regularly in different parts of the forest that overlooked West Sedge Moor. Hidden in some small clearing, with a thick canopy of green overhead, fallen logs for benches and a tree stump for a pulpit, or even a communion table, that small group of men and women experienced times when the presence of God seemed so close that his nearness was almost tangible. And when Pastor Bartlett preached on the words which Christ had spoken shortly before his crucifixion, 'In the world ye shall have tribulation: but be of good cheer; I have overcome the world,'[2] all present felt a new surge of joy and strength. Even if they were called upon to suffer, Christ would conquer, and his strength would sustain them through the darkest times. As Emma edged closer to Robert on their log bench, with little Alice on her lap and her second baby due shortly, she felt an unexpected peace of heart, a fresh confidence in the overruling power of God that had eluded her for so long.

But dangers abounded. The woods were regularly patrolled by soldiers ever vigilant to discover groups of secret worshippers. Two or three members of the congregation were always posted at vantage points where they could keep a careful watch for approaching danger. At a given signal — a short sharp whistle — the congregation would disband in an instant, melting into the surrounding woodland, clambering into prearranged hiding places, until a further signal indicated that the danger had passed.

But one Sunday morning towards the end of September when a low mist hung over the woods, Robert had an uneasy sense of trouble ahead. With their second child born only two weeks previously — a fair-haired little boy named James in memory of Robert's brother — Emma remained at home with Nicholas, who was too frail to scramble among the trees, too slow to make any escape should the need arise. Kissing Emma goodbye and giving his small daughter Alice an enthusiastic hug, Robert set off alone.

All seemed quiet as he rode along, before harnessing his horse securely to a tree at the edge of the forest and continuing on foot, thrusting his way through tangled undergrowth, deep among the trees. At last he reached the prearranged meeting place. Twenty or more had already arrived, and so Robert found a place to sit at the back of the group. Soon the service began: prayer, Scripture, a message; but no singing was possible, for that would quickly betray their location.

Today they were to celebrate the Lord's Supper together, and as the small loaf of bread was passed round, followed by a flagon of wine, Robert became acutely aware of the love that bound together these hunted believers, both to each other and to the Saviour, a man of sorrows, acquainted with grief.

'Trust in the Lord, at all times, you people, pour out your heart before him: God is a refuge for us.' Francis Bartlett's clear commanding voice rang out with assurance and hope as he closed the service with the words of the fugitive King David.[3] His tall figure slightly stooped with age, his auburn hair now streaked with grey, Bartlett had been a fine and faithful pastor for many years. His wife had died some years earlier, and as Robert looked at him with affection, he wondered how much longer he could bear the strain of leadership under such conditions.

Just as the small group prepared to scatter and return to their homes, the air was suddenly filled with ugly sounds of yelling coming from all sides at once. Unnoticed by those appointed to keep a lookout, a number of armed men had been silently surrounding them and were now rushing in. But with equally quick movements the worshippers were disappearing among the trees, slipping in and out until out of sight. This was a well-practised drill. Robert turned to run, but at that moment he felt a firm grip on his arm and the sharp point of a bayonet thrust into the small of his back. He was caught.

Frogmarched all the way back to the town hall, together with two other men whom the soldiers had managed to grab, Robert wondered wildly about Emma, about his old father. What would happen if he were thrown into prison? How would he pay a five-pound fine? Perhaps it would be better to undertake to return to the parish church, no matter how wrong the *Book of Common Prayer* might be. God would understand his predicament. Surely his family ought to take first place in his life? So many thoughts flooded his mind in that long harsh walk back to Langport that Robert could hardly tell which were his own and which were subtly whispered into his mind by Satan, that arch-enemy of truth.

And still Emma waited. Where could Robert be? He should have been home an hour ago. His meal had gone cold; his father Nicholas was pacing backwards and forwards, constantly peering out of the window, and even little Alice seemed to sense that something was wrong.

Morning turned to afternoon and gradually the September sun sank to the west; the air grew chilly as darkness began to gather. Nicholas went out to attend to the needs of the farm, but it was almost too much for him now.

Then came the crunching sound of a horse's hooves along the path, followed by a knock at the door. Pastor Bartlett stooped as he entered the low farmhouse doorway and seated himself at the kitchen table. Concern was written on his face. 'I am afraid to tell you,' he began, but Emma had guessed and buried her head in her hands. At last she looked up tearfully. 'What's happened?'

'They have taken Robert to Ilchester Jail until he agrees to pay the fine. The king's soldiers surprised us as we were finishing our worship. Robert, Josiah Wyatt and John Williams were all taken. I have just come from the prison myself and can tell you that your husband bears up nobly; his whole concern is for you and his family.'

'What shall I do?' asked Emma, her voice breaking with anxiety. Alice began to wail and Nicholas came and stood with his arm around his daughter-in-law.

'We will cast them upon our God in prayer,' said Pastor Bartlett, 'and remember, Emma, the words of our Saviour: "Let not your heart be troubled, neither let it be afraid." '[4]

When Francis Bartlett rose to go, Emma looked up with a tearful smile, and shook his hand warmly. She even managed to snatch a little sleep that night, and as she nursed baby James during the small hours of the morning she was able to commit her infants' father, her dearly loved husband, to the God whose promises had never failed her.

16.
WHEN DEATH STALKED THE CITY

'I have been talking to Papa,' said Robert, 'and we have decided it is best to sell up the livestock on the farm.' Emma listened in silence, only too glad to have Robert back at home. For two days he had been kept a prisoner at Ilchester. For hour after hour a panel of local magistrates had bombarded him with questions, depriving him of sleep. Where did they usually meet? How many were present at their services? Who was preaching on the occasion of his arrest? And still Robert remained silent. At last, knowing how much his family needed him, he agreed to pay the five-pound fine, levied for a first offence against the Conventicle Act.

'It could be ten pounds next time,' he told Emma with a wry smile.

'But how shall we live?' asked Emma anxiously.

'The printing press has been doing well, and I can expand it and get some extra local help, perhaps employ another man or two,' replied Robert. 'And, besides, Papa is too old to manage the farm if anything should happen to me. Although he is sad to lose the livestock, he has now agreed to the sale.'

As Robert waited for the Taunton auction to begin, he watched with a pang of regret as the Romney sheep his family had bred over many years bleated and jostled together in the pens. A highly prized breed with long, superior-quality wool, the animals were in excellent condition. 'They should fetch a good price,' thought Robert to himself. Nor was he disappointed. The sale of the farm stock not only enabled him to pay the five-pound fine — equivalent to a year's wage for a farmhand — but to invest in an extra, and updated, printing press to expand his business.

Following the arrests in the forest, the small congregation of the Langport Independent Church soon found that there were watchful eyes everywhere. Who could tell whether some innocent-looking bystander was actually noting down every movement of a known church member? Social status was to be gained from information leading to a successful prosecution; even some financial benefits could result. While the weather was favourable, the forest was still the safest place to meet. And one of Robert's tasks was to search out new locations, always ensuring that there were some escape routes, either further into the forest or out onto the moors should trouble arise.

As winter set in, with a thick gleaming blanket of snow covering the fields, the forest could no longer be used. Not only would the piercing barbs of icy winds penetrate the thin coats of many of the poorer people who gathered, but the telltale tracks in the snow were easy to follow. Well-trodden paths to barns, outhouses and even cattle-sheds must now be used instead, and many a strange meeting place was transformed into a sanctuary where God met his people — a hunted band of Christian men and women who worshipped him there. And always they had to be on the alert for informers, either spying from a distance or even using more subtle means of deception — pretending to have spiritual concerns in order to conceal their baser motives.

Not far from Moorside Farm on the banks of the River Parrett stood a derelict house. Only approachable through dense woodland, it had once been the home of a wealthy merchant, but was now overgrown with brambles, eerie and long deserted. Strange stories circulated about the fate

The deserted house

of its owner. Some said that he had fallen into the river in an inebriated condition and perished; others that he had been murdered, his body dumped in the river and his house vandalized. Whatever the truth, no one dared approach the old house, particularly at night. Here, then, was an ideal spot to meet, and after overcoming their initial fears the members of the Langport meeting found it a safe haven where they could gather unmolested by the constant fear of informers.

At last came the spring of 1665; the snows had retreated and a spirit of growing optimism was abroad, for no further disturbances had occurred. Joseph Alleine had been freed from prison. Little Alice, nearly two, followed her mother everywhere with an endless stream of scarcely intelligible questions. Their only concern was Nicholas' health. He seemed to be drifting further and further into a world of his own. The loss of the farm livestock had proved another emotional setback for him and although Emma often spent time reading to him, or would place baby James playfully on his lap, he showed little interest. Sometimes he spoke about his own son James, mown down by fleeing horsemen after the Battle of Langport; often he spoke of his wife, Alice.

Robert had built an extension to Moorside Farm where he had installed his new printing press. Work was coming in steadily and the excellent standard and reliability of Robert's productions had gained the press a good reputation over a wide area. His new employee, a local lad named Sammy Coates, was a quick learner and Robert soon handed over much of the routine work to the fourteen-year-old. From a good background, Sammy had hoped to set himself up in business as a blacksmith, but the sudden death of his father had reduced the family to poverty. With three younger brothers, anything Sammy earned had to go straight to his mother to feed the family. Although the boy was able enough at his work, he nursed a dark resentment against his lot in life.

Emma found herself less than happy about Robert's young employee. She hardly knew why, but sometimes when she entered the workshop unexpectedly she had noticed a look on Sammy's face that troubled her. The discontented curl of his lip, with a restive, perhaps even mean and envious, look in his eyes, suggested that there were two sides to Sammy Coates. 'Are you sure you can trust Sammy?' she asked Robert one day.

'Trust him? Why, of course I can! He's hardworking and honest,' Robert replied in surprise. Emma said no more. Perhaps she was wrong.

Then one June day an exhausted horse with a travel-stained rider cantered up the drive. Hurrying to the door, Emma gasped in astonishment. None other than Hugh Wilmot was dismounting. Excitedly Emma rushed into the workshop to summon Robert, but in her haste she had not noticed the strained and sad expression on Hugh's face. Robert saw it immediately. 'What's the matter?' he asked anxiously.

'You have not heard?' asked Hugh gently.

'Why, no. Is all well with you?'

'The Black Death! The Black Death has come! All London trembles!' exclaimed Hugh. 'The king has fled to Oxford; so too has Parliament. Fear haunts every street; the death toll mounts daily with thousands swept to the grave. And those crosses, those dreadful red crosses that are painted on every door where the plague is raging within!

Houses are barricaded from the outside so that none may come out nor any go in, other than those appointed to do so. The markets are deserted… Each day the death cart patrols the streets, calling on all to bring out their dead for burial in the vast communal graves now being dug.'

'Mama and Papa! Are they safe?' gasped Emma.

'I warned them to flee,' continued Hugh in a low voice. 'Most assuredly I did. But your father would have none of it. He says he must finish some printing he is doing, although he urged your mother and brothers to come to you for safety.'

Emma buried her face in her hands. 'And the plague? Has it reached them?'

'I fear so,' answered Hugh quietly. 'I rode by the Sign of the Morning Star three days ago and…'

'The red cross! Oh, was the red cross on their door too?' interrupted Emma.

Hugh could only nod in reply, adding, 'But whether your parents and brothers are still alive, I cannot say. I set out that very day and have ridden hard these many miles that I might warn you.'

Emma could bear no more, but rushed from the room. 'Will you not stay with us, my good friend?' said Robert kindly. 'I fear lest you too should take the illness.'

'No, no, I will not stay, in case I carry the fearsome plague on my clothing. But I will keep watch on Bernard and Sarah's home and hope to return to tell you all I know.'

Just as he was about to remount his horse, Hugh was distracted by small arms clinging to his leg. Looking down he saw a dark-eyed child gazing up at him. 'And this must be your little daughter,' he smiled. Alice raised her arms to

Hugh asking to be lifted: it was almost as if she knew he was a well-loved friend. Swinging the child high in the air, Hugh laughed, gave her a quick hug and rode off, refusing both rest and refreshment. 'I'll be back,' he said briefly.

Two long and tortuous weeks passed. 'If they are still alive, they may well recover,' Robert suggested, trying to reassure Emma. She merely shook her head sadly, and Robert was grateful that the care of her two children occupied much of her time.

Then at last Hugh returned. But Emma knew he brought heavy news even before he spoke. 'Which is it?' she asked pointedly.

'Your mother and your brother Thomas are well,' replied Hugh, trying to break the news as compassionately as he could.

'Where have they buried Papa and Tim?' asked Emma forlornly.

'Because they worshipped at an Independent church, I saw their bodies being taken to Bunhill Fields, in the village of Islington, where there is a graveyard in unconsecrated ground. Many are being buried there,' answered Hugh. There was no easy way to break such news to Emma.

'Can you arrange for Mama and Tom to come to us?' asked Emma, still too stunned to take in the full import of all that Hugh was saying.

'I have already done so,' he replied, 'and they will come as soon as they are permitted to leave. They will need much support, I fear.'

Hugh agreed to stay a day or two with the family. He had finished the first part of his law studies and was soon to begin his final training as a barrister. For hours he sat beside Nicholas, the one to whom he owed his life. The old man's only consolation seemed to be found in the pages of his worn old Bible. With failing eyesight, he often asked Hugh to read to him. Disinclined to do so at first, Hugh obliged for the sake of the debt he owed. But one day Nicholas asked him to read Psalm 23. Hugh struggled through the verses: 'Yea, though I walk through the valley of the shadow of death, I will fear no evil...' Then he came to the last verse: 'Surely goodness and mercy shall follow me all the days of my life...' He could go no further. Snapping the book shut, he hurried from the room. 'How can you say that "goodness and mercy have followed you"?' he stormed to Robert. 'Your brother is dead; your mother was burned to death; you are a hunted man; Emma's father and brother are dead. And what about me? Just look at my scarred face! And what about my beloved Samile and my infant son? He didn't even have a name. You can't expect me to believe that!'

Robert wisely did not comment, knowing that his friend needed time to calm down. Just at that moment little Alice wandered into the room, holding out her hand for Hugh to take her for a walk. Grasping the small hand in his, Hugh limped out into the June sunshine.

17.
DANGERS PAST ... DANGERS PRESENT

Three weeks later, when the risk of further infection had passed, Sarah Allen and her remaining son, Thomas, hired a wagon, packed up many of their possessions and set off for Somerset. It took five days before the small wagon eventually rumbled down the path leading to Moorside Farm. Emma was shocked to see how thin and tired her mother looked, while Thomas, soon to be twenty-three, who had been inseparable from his twin brother, had a haunted, bitter look in his eyes that troubled his older sister.

The peaceful countryside, the meadows starred with buttercups and the gleam of the distant river among the trees breathed an atmosphere of calm after the trauma of recent weeks. For Sarah, her grandchildren's cheerful presence, with baby James beginning to crawl everywhere, brought a measure of healing. But for Thomas nothing appeared to bring relief. His face seemed set — a stricken, distraught blank. He scarcely spoke and ate little. Robert gave him work to do in the press, knowing that the diversion could take his mind off his loss and the ghastly scenes of suffering and death that he had witnessed.

Before long Thomas began to give himself to the printing work with an intensity that astonished Robert. He could hardly keep both Sammy Coates and Thomas fully occupied, so quickly did Thomas finish any task set him. But his frenetic energy seemed unnatural. More problematic was the fact that Sammy clearly resented the newcomer's presence. 'Perhaps he fears he may lose his job,' thought Robert.

But gradually Robert discovered something else that perturbed him deeply: he was receiving a steady stream of rejected work returned to him — something that had rarely if ever happened before. At last he was forced to look more closely into the situation and traced the errors to the work of his younger employee. Sammy was deliberately introducing mistakes, even sabotaging important documents. Twice Robert faced the youth with the complaints and made him repeat the work, but the boy just looked sullen, and still the problems continued. At last Robert was forced to dismiss him. With an inscrutable look on his face, Sammy Coates walked out of the Moorside Printing Works as if nothing had happened, but somehow Robert knew that he might well seek his revenge one day. Perhaps Emma had been right about him after all.

Weekends proved particularly difficult with Thomas. While Sarah was happy to join in the services of worship, frequently held in the deserted house with its echoing gloomy rooms, or alternatively to sit with Nicholas and the children so that Emma could attend, Thomas was far from willing. On Sundays he would disappear for long hours at a time. Where he went, he would never divulge. But the strong smell of alcohol on his breath and his somewhat erratic behaviour on his return gave the family all the information they needed.

'I shall be moving away shortly,' Thomas announced one Sunday night in September. 'I plan to marry, but I will still work for you at the press.'

A look of blank astonishment marked each face around the family supper table. Everyone stared at the young man in total disbelief. Then Nicholas, who did not often speak, broke the silence. 'And who do you plan to marry, young man?'

'No one you know,' Thomas replied evenly. All eyes were fixed on him. Clearly he had to say more. 'A young woman — dark-eyed and beautiful — whom I have been meeting every Sunday at the Black Bull tavern in town.'

'Named?' prompted Robert.

'Named Nelly, Nelly Smeaton, but you would not know her, a high-class girl — not the sort that people like you would mix with.' With a venomous sting, even a double meaning in his words, Thomas waited for a reaction, but there was little that anyone could say. Certainly Robert did not wish his mother-in-law or Thomas to know of his previous indiscretion involving the Smeaton family when he had foolishly printed *The Freeman Chronicles*, airing the nobility's anti-government propaganda.

'And when do you plan to marry this woman?' asked Robert eventually, hardly knowing what else to say.

'Very soon,' came the reply. 'We will celebrate in six weeks' time. Nelly is older than I am and we do not want to wait. We plan to live in Pibsbury.'

The shock of her son's unexpected announcement was a clear setback for Sarah. How could he behave like that when they had both suffered so much together? She did not mind him marrying, but to announce it like that and with the wedding so soon was hurtful and inconsiderate. Emma often sat with her mother, who wept as if bereaved for a second time, until at last she came to realize that the loss of his twin brother in such circumstances was at the root of Thomas's unpredictable behaviour. Perhaps if she could learn to love and accept Nelly, whose family had also suffered, she could come to terms with the situation.

When Thomas first introduced his bride-to-be to the family her black eyes flashed with suppressed laughter as she recognized Robert. But flighty and conceited though she was, she had no wish to resurrect the past. She knew well that Robert had paid a high price for obliging her family and decided to say nothing — at least not for the present. The wedding, however, was a quiet one, for Earl and Lady Smeaton, who had strong High Church sympathies, clearly disapproved of their only daughter marrying below her station in life, and especially into a family that refused to attend the local parish church.

A far darker shadow rested on the small group of Christians who met each week under the preaching of Francis Bartlett. Many in the country interpreted the terrible death toll resulting from the Great Plague, put by some at 100,000, as God's judgement on a wicked government which persecuted upright and godly men and women. But the Cavalier Parliament thought differently.

No sooner had the worst of the outbreak eased than Parliament voted through another repressive law against Nonconformist preachers.

Some London pastors had returned to their pulpits during the epidemic to support the people in their need. This new law, known as the Five Mile Act, was passed in order to prohibit such a thing ever happening again. No ejected preacher would be allowed to live or minister within five miles of his former church. A crippling fine of £40 was the penalty imposed on any who were discovered breaking the law. Not only had these conscientious men been deprived of both church and income, now many of them would lose their homes as well. Joseph Alleine and his loyal wife Theodosia were among the first to feel the impact of this harsh legislation as they were forbidden to live within five miles of Taunton. Now they were obliged to wander from place to place staying with anyone who was able to accommodate them.

With their marriage that November, Thomas and Nelly were now living in Pibsbury, leaving Thomas's room at Moorside Farm empty. Not long afterwards Robert asked Emma a question, the answer to which could be very costly: 'Would you be willing for me to ask Mr Alleine and his wife to stay with us if ever they should require the shelter?' He scarcely needed an answer. Although Emma knew the risk, knew the brutal treatment meted out to anyone discovered giving sanctuary to Joseph Alleine, she was prepared to take her share of the danger and sufferings. She merely nodded.

'Instead of my one home, I now have a hundred different homes,' said Alleine cheerfully, as he thanked Robert for the kind offer. Since his release from prison continual warrants had been issued for his arrest, for he insisted on preaching wherever he found people willing to listen. With the passing of this new law he dared not remain long in any one place for fear of arrest. Many a time the fugitive pastor could be found slipping out of the back door while soldiers were hammering at the front. Entering, they would slash through the curtains with their swords, thrust their weapons into beds and up chimneys searching for Alleine, eventually to leave empty-handed in disgust. Perhaps at that very moment the hunted man was lying under bales of hay in some outhouse, or stealing in and out of the trees in nearby woods.

By March 1666, the brutal winter temperatures were slowly easing and a lone blackbird was singing hopefully not far from Emma's kitchen window at Moorside Farm. The gleaming ice on the River Parrett was beginning to thaw, and both Robert and Emma were feeling a new measure of optimism. Joseph and Theodosia Alleine had been staying at Moorside for almost two weeks, and had only left the previous night, for it was safer to travel in the dark. Just before they rode away Alleine had gathered the family together, all standing around the tattered armchair where Nicholas always chose to sit. With one arm on the old man's shoulder and the other around little Alice, who was perched on the arm of the chair, Alleine spoke seriously to them all about the privileges of suffering for Christ and his gospel. It seemed almost as if he knew that they might yet pay a heavy price for their kindness to him. His words were ones that Robert and Emma would never forget:

I have no doubt that the God of mercy has yet more choice blessings in store for you. Do not be weakened

Moorland track at dusk

*by my sufferings. What is a candle for, but to be
burned? And as for me, I have received nothing but
good at the hands of the Lord all my days. So be strong
in the Lord, my dear friends; fear not your adversaries,
for they can only harm your bodies, but may not touch
your souls.*

Then he and his wife were gone — riding out into the
gloom of a March night. Where they were going, the family
did not know, for ignorance of their whereabouts could be
a mercy in these circumstances.

But someone saw them go. Randolph Bilton, the local
barber-surgeon, known colloquially as Randy Cut-throat,
was on his way home after a day's work. The coins he had
earned that day jingled cheerfully in the pocket of his
breeches. As he thought of the crude surgery he had just

performed, he shrugged his shoulders. He cared little whether his patient lived or died, as long as he received his fees. As he passed the end of the lane leading to Moorside Farm he found his mind wandering back to that injured soldier all those years ago and the way Nicholas Wilkes had dispensed with his services when he offered to amputate the man's leg. He spat in disgust at the remembrance.

Just at that moment he had to rein in his horse sharply for he had nearly collided with two figures, heavily cloaked, riding swiftly and silently away from the farm. Who could they be? Randy Cut-throat thought quickly. Like everyone else in Langport, he had heard of the preaching of Joseph Alleine and knew he was a hunted man. He knew too that the Wilkes family were members of the Independent church that was now forbidden to gather. The two strands of thought joined in his pitiless mind as he rattled the coins in his pocket together. Why, here was an opportunity not just to inform on Nicholas Wilkes and his family, but to track the fugitives, who by now were some way ahead of him! A double reward maybe?

With a loud crack of his whip, he urged his old horse forward, intent on following the two riders to discover where they were going to stay. But the night was dark and icy potholes pitted the lane. Unexpectedly his animal skidded helplessly under him and landed heavily on its knees. Cursing volubly, Bilton dismounted, dragged the hapless creature to its feet and tried to inspect the injury. Clearly it was in pain. Now he would have to lead the horse slowly home. Any chance of following Mr Alleine and his wife had vanished. But at least he knew where they had been.

18.
BETRAYED

When a courier from London arrived at Moorside and delivered a letter for Robert, addressed to him in a spidery hand, Robert smiled to himself. 'Why, it's from Hugh Wilmot,' he told Emma, 'a strange event indeed!' Stamped with thick red sealing wax, and bearing Hugh's personal logo, the letter was dated 22 March 1666. Robert's smile broadened as he tried to decipher the closely written lines, for Hugh's handwriting was quite illegible in places. Emma stood at his side, anxiously waiting for news. Yes, Hugh was well, Robert reported; in fact he was writing to say that he had finally completed his legal studies at Gray's Inn and had recently been called to the Bar. He hoped to be promoted quickly, for his rank as the nephew of Henry Wilmot, Earl of Rochester, had put him in a unique position. In addition, he was able to obtain personal access to King Charles himself at any time as a reward for the services his uncle had rendered when Charles had been wandering from place to place as an exile during the Commonwealth period.

Then, almost as a postscript to his letter, Hugh added that he had recently been reading a very strange book — newly published and evidently selling fast — a religious book written by someone who had spent the last six years as a prisoner in Bedford Jail. Hugh understood that the writer, a man called John Bunyan, was suffering for the same sort of beliefs that Robert and his family held. And the book, Hugh continued, had the most surprising title: *Grace Abounding to the Chief of Sinners.* Evidently, this writer — just a common tinker — had been a godless character: wild, abandoned and a prolific blasphemer. 'But I cannot put the book down,' Hugh admitted, 'for this fellow, John Bunyan, relates the oddest story of how he became religious.'

One sentence above others had struck him, Hugh told Robert. As the prisoner described his journey from being a coarse blasphemer to a man prepared to endure prison and death for his beliefs, he said, 'The Bible became precious to me in those days.' 'Those words,' Hugh confessed, 'brought tears to my eyes, because I could almost see your papa sitting there by candlelight, reading that old Bible of his. I know that he would agree with John Bunyan, for the book certainly seems precious to him too.' Then Hugh added (and Robert had to read it again carefully to make sure he had understood correctly), 'It almost makes me wonder if I could ever change like that.'

Right at the end of the letter Hugh wrote, 'In spite of my success, I am lonely here. Perhaps I could visit you again before long. Give little Alice a hug from me.'

GRACE

Abounding to the chief of Sinners:

OR,
A Brief and Faithful

RELATION

Of the Exceeding Mercy of God in Chrift, to his poor Servant

JOHN BUNYAN.

Wherein is particularly fhewed, The manner of his Converfion, his fight and trouble for Sin, his Dreadful Temptations, alfo how he defpaired of Gods mercy, and how the Lord at length thorow Chrift did deliver him from all the guilt and terrour that lay upon him.

Whereunto is added,

A brief Relation of his Call to the Work of the Miniftry, of his Temptations therein, as alfo what he hath met with in Prifon.

All which was written by his own hand there, and now publifhed for the fupport of the weak and tempted People of God.

Come and hear, all ye that fear God ; and I will declare what he hath done for my foul, Pfal. 66. 16.

LONDON:
Printed by *George Larkin*. 1666.

Title-page of the 1666 edition of John Bunyan's *Grace Abounding to the Chief of Sinners*

'What a letter!' said Robert as he handed the closely written page to Emma for her to read it for herself. Even though Emma's third baby was due in July, she was delighted to know that Hugh might be able to come and stay.

Emma was not the only one expecting a child. No one was surprised when Nelly and Thomas announced, somewhat shamefacedly, that Nelly was also pregnant, her baby expected in May — only six months after their marriage. And Nelly was frightened. She had never been strong, and her pregnancy had been far from easy. Her mother, Lady Smeaton, had distanced herself yet further from Nelly when she discovered the situation. Her daughter's marriage had been offence enough; this only added to the shame Nelly had brought on their proud family name.

Sarah was different. Unlike Thomas, her sufferings had given her a new tenderness. Instead of censuring Nelly and Thomas, she had shown an unexpected concern for her new daughter-in-law. Day after day she walked the mile or more to Pibsbury, often along frozen tracks, to sit with Nelly and gain her confidence. Many women died in childbirth, a fact that both knew well. 'What if I should die?' Nelly ventured at last, voicing her inmost fears. 'I have behaved badly, I know, and done many wrong things. I think God will reject me.' Sarah tried to calm Nelly's fears, but at the same time pointed her to the God of mercy who would forgive the penitent. Thomas listened patiently to his mother's words; he too knew the answers, but felt unable to say anything to Nelly.

Then at three o'clock on a bitterly cold April morning, Robert and Emma were woken by a frantic hammering on the kitchen door. It was Thomas. Nelly had gone into premature labour and was calling out for Sarah. Throwing a rough cloak around her shoulders, Sarah, still bleary with sleep, rode pillion on her son's horse to Pibsbury. The midwife, grumbling bitterly at the night-time emergency, had already arrived, but when Nelly saw Sarah she clung desperately to her hand like a frightened child — all the bravado of her earlier years seemed to have vanished. Long hours of labour passed, with the midwife's face growing ever more gloomy.

At last, as the weak April sun shone into the room, a tiny baby girl was born. Sarah wrapped the frail mite in a blanket and put her in Nelly's arms, but as she did so the tears were streaming down her face. Nelly was exhausted, but even she could see that her baby's grasp on life was fragile at best. 'We will call her Annie,' was her only comment. And by evening of that same day little Annie's spirit had fled, leaving Thomas and Nelly broken and desolate. Even Lady Smeaton called to see her daughter and offered what consolation she could, but it had a hollow ring. Day after day Sarah came across to Pibsbury to care for Nelly, until Thomas suggested that his mother should come to live with them until Nelly had regained her strength.

During those days the small and frequently hounded group of Christians who made up the membership of the Langport Meeting continued to worship in different locations. The old deserted house by the river remained the safest place to meet, but for Emma's sake, whose third child was due in early July, and for old Nicholas, who was increasingly infirm, they occasionally took the risk of gathering at Moorside Farm. Not only did it afford plenty of space, but the meadows, the moors and even the deep winding rhyne provided escape routes in case of need.

Danger was in the air. That very month Joseph Alleine, together with seven other preachers and forty members of their congregations and friends, had been brutally arrested, charged with breaking the Conventicle Act and marched off to Ilchester once again. Robert was deeply concerned for Alleine, as he had been seriously ill in recent weeks with a type of paralysis that affected the use of his arms. He could eat little and had lost much weight. But, despite this, nothing could dissuade the earnest pastor from preaching wherever he could.

Thomas, and even Nelly, had begun to attend the gatherings for worship from time to time, particularly when they were held at the farm. Emma noticed that as her brother and his wife listened to Francis Bartlett's searching preaching and his urgent exhortations to faith and courage, a new tenderness was beginning to creep into Nelly's rather hardened face, a dawning understanding perhaps. Nelly's unselfish joy when Emma's third child — a second son whom they called Philip — was born in July, was another sign of the improvement in the younger woman's disposition.

Never were the services held at the same time each week — sometimes the group would meet before the first streaks of dawn lightened the night sky; on other occasions it would be at the dead of night, and all in an attempt to avoid the prying eyes of any would-be informer. But after one such occasion Thomas asked Robert a strange question when he came to work: 'Have you been using the services of Randolph Bilton, the barber-surgeon, here recently?'

Robert threw back his head and roared with laughter. 'Randy Cut-throat? Do you really think I would?'

But Thomas was not laughing. 'On two or three occasions I have seen him and that poor old nag of his hanging round the lanes when I have been coming to work or going home, and even yesterday I am sure I saw him hiding among the trees beside the lane. I fear he may be up to no good, perhaps checking on those who visit Moorside.' Robert did not laugh this time.

When they next met everyone was on special alert. All was quiet. But only two days later, as the Wilkes family had just finished supper on a hot evening late in July, and were still gathered round the table, a threatening sound of marching feet could be heard in the lane. Robert leaped up in alarm, but at that moment three armed men burst in through the open door, waving their swords and shouting at the frightened family. Alice fled behind her mother for protection; two-year-old James began to let out ear-piercing yells, while the new baby joined in the general commotion.

'We are arresting you, old man,' said one burly soldier above the din, shaking Nicholas roughly, 'for sheltering that law-breaking preacher, Joseph Alleine.'

'And you, sir,' said another, brandishing his sword in Robert's face, 'you are under arrest for holding illegal conventicles in this house.'

'And may I ask what evidence you have for such an accusation?' demanded Robert without raising his voice.

'Evidence, sir, evidence? Why none but the very best, and that on many occasions!' A look of fear crept into Robert's clear blue eyes, as the soldier continued. 'A worthy citizen by the name of Bilton, Mr Randolph Bilton, deeply concerned for the honour of His Majesty the King and for the just laws of this realm, was constrained to mention his unease about your activities to the Clerk of the Justices of the Peace in Taunton.'

'And you may leave my old father alone,' snapped Robert. 'As for this Bilton, he has not crossed the threshold of our home for more than twenty years.'

All argument was useless as the soldier dragged Nicholas to his feet, pushing him towards the door. 'You will not do so!' cried Emma in alarm, throwing herself in the doorway. Thrusting her roughly to one side, the third soldier leered mockingly at the young woman saying, 'And you be grateful, madam, that we do not have orders to take you as well.' With that, both father and son were unceremoniously bundled out of the house and marched off down the lane, Nicholas stumbling as he went.

Leaning heavily on Robert's arm, Nicholas staggered along the rough lanes, goaded on by a soldier on horseback. Ilchester lay ten miles away, and Robert knew that his father could never walk that distance. Each time he stopped to regain his breath the impatient soldier poked him in the back with his sword. At this rate of progress they would not be there until after midnight.

'You must let my father ride,' shouted Robert, but a coarse laugh was the only response. Then, without warning, Nicholas suddenly slumped by the roadside, too exhausted to take another step. Swear as much as he would, the accompanying soldier could not get the old man to his feet. Robert sat down beside him. 'Papa,' he said, 'take a drink from my bottle of water.' At last, seeing that Nicholas could go no further, the soldier dismounted and heaved Nicholas up into the saddle. Even so, progress was painfully slow, and finally the party was obliged to spend the night at a wayside inn, before resuming the long walk in the morning.

By the time they arrived, the temperature in the upper day room, the Bridewell Chamber, was steadily rising and Nicholas was at the point of collapse — their only joy to see their well-loved friend, Joseph Alleine. Despite his physical weakness he was about to conduct a service for his fellow prisoners. So, finding a space on the floor, Robert laid his father carefully down on a straw mat, and sat nearby to listen. Nicholas had slipped into semi-consciousness.

19.
A PROMISE KEPT

When Hugh Wilmot entered King Charles II's lavish court at Whitehall, even he was astounded at the luxury, but appalled by the decadence surrounding the monarch. The first thing that struck him, as he paused to take in his surroundings, was the foul doggish smell that wafted across the marbled courtroom; the next, the sharp yapping of the king's three favourite spaniels that rushed forward to greet the stranger. Singing girls started giggling in the background at Hugh's obvious dislike of the animals, but Charles himself, ar-rayed in gorgeous silks, his long, curling black wig cascading down his

King Charles II

shoulders, was more engrossed with his most recent mistress, Moll Davis, sitting at his feet, than with any affair of court.

'Your Majesty,' said Hugh, dropping on one knee. Tearing his eyes momentarily away from Moll's pretty babyish face, Charles glanced at Hugh. Then he looked again.

'Why, if it is not Hugh Wilmot!' he exclaimed. 'And how are you, my scarred-faced young friend?'

Ignoring the insult, Hugh said calmly, 'If your Majesty pleases, may I have a word with you in private?' Rising from his stately seat, Charles withdrew from the noise and laughter of the courtroom and Hugh followed him.

'Many years have passed since we roamed the Continent together and your good uncle ...', the king began pleasantly. Then he broke off suddenly: 'And how is that young barmaid you married?'

Again Hugh swallowed hard and tried to answer without betraying his emotions: 'I fear she died in childbirth, Your Majesty, but I come to you today on behalf of another — one to whom I owe my life.'

'And who may that be?' asked the king, suddenly interested.

'One who rescued me as I lay dying after the Battle of Langport, even at the expense of his own son's life.'

The king's face darkened at the memory of that battle, crucial in the defeat of the Royalist forces. 'Oliver Cromwell, curse him!' he muttered under his breath as Hugh thrust a neatly written letter into the king's hand. The letter was from Emma sent to Hugh in much distress as she explained their situation and begged him to help her if he possibly could.

'Farmer Nicholas Wilkes, now a frail old man,' continued Hugh, 'lies dying in Your Majesty's jail at Ilchester and for no crime whatsoever.'

''Tis true?' asked the king. 'And of what is he accused?'

'Your Majesty, he and his noble son, my friend, were betrayed by one Randolph Bilton, a barber-surgeon, as an act of revenge, for the man Bilton would have amputated my leg — his skill being little and his saw but rusty. Having rescued me from certain death, this good farmer intervened for me at great cost to his own livelihood...'

'Betrayed, betrayed, was he? And for what?' demanded the king, raising his voice.

'For sheltering an honest and homeless priest who in no way broke the laws of Your Majesty's realm.'

The king pursed his lips in thought; clearly the matter lay in the balance, and so Hugh continued boldly, 'The old man now lies near to death, Your Majesty, in a prison both vile and full beyond capacity, and his son, arrested with him, is an innocent man with three small children dependent upon him.'

'And are such things done in my land?' roared the king, who despite his dissolute lifestyle knew what it was to be harried and hounded by his enemies. Then, turning over Emma's letter, he wrote on the back in large letters:

Free Nicholas Wilkes and his son immediately upon my personal orders, and fine the man Bilton for all the expense suffered by the state for his actions.
                                                            Charles Rex

Then he handed the letter back to Hugh, and rose to go, for he was eager to return to Moll's company.

'I thank Your Gracious Majesty for your kindness,' said Hugh with a final bow.

'And may I recommend,' responded the king with a sly smile, 'a visit to an east of London theatre? For there, like me, you may find many a pretty barmaid, or even an actress or two to suit your tastes.'

Hugh scowled inwardly, but merely said once more, 'I owe my thanks to Your Majesty,' bowed again and made his way back through the court, past the yapping dogs and the scantily dressed singing girls, and breathed the fresh air again with relief.

As Hugh saddled his fastest horse to ride to Ilchester, a wild confusion of thoughts was racing through his mind. Two far different scenes flashed before him. He saw an old man, poring over the tattered pages of an open Bible, muttering to himself, 'Yea, though I walk through the valley of the shadow of death, I will fear no evil...' This scene was quickly replaced by one of a shameless young woman basking in the attentions of an immoral king amid all the extravagance of a royal courtroom. Now Hugh knew at last which he preferred.

If Hugh was taken aback by the disagreeable smell of dogs at Whitehall, the stench that greeted his nostrils as he climbed the stairs up to the Bridewell Chamber in Ilchester Jail on his arrival three days later almost overpowered him. He stepped gingerly over rows of prisoners, some lying on their mats, others trying to occupy the long hours by reading or talking to friends, for many had been arrested at the same gathering as Joseph Alleine. Then Hugh spotted the fair head of his friend Robert bent low over a prostrate figure on the floor.

One glance at Nicholas Wilkes's still white face told Hugh that the old man had already passed through the 'valley of the shadow of death'. The last words of that psalm — words that Hugh had been unable to read to him those months ago — had come true for Nicholas. Surely he was now 'dwelling in the house of the LORD for ever'. Kneeling down beside Robert, Hugh placed one arm around his shoulders — his own sorrow making it impossible for him to speak.

'I'm too late,' he said at last, 'too late.' He pulled Emma's letter from the pocket of his breeches and showed Robert the king's message. Robert merely nodded dumbly and squeezed Hugh's hand in appreciation. At that moment he recalled that many years ago, when he and Hugh had first parted after the Battle of Langport, Hugh had said, 'One day, perhaps I can repay you for your kindness and for the loss of your brother's life.' And today he had done just that.

Leaving Robert for the moment, Hugh went to make arrangements for Robert's immediate discharge and for Nicholas' body to be taken home to be buried beside his wife Alice. When he returned he discovered a serious-looking man in earnest conversation with Robert. 'Hugh,' interrupted Robert, 'meet my friend Mr Joseph Alleine.'

'I have heard much about you, good sir, said Hugh solemnly, as he shook the slender white hand stretched out to greet him. Privately he could not help noticing how ill Mr Alleine looked — and little wonder in such a place. 'If I can I will do all in my power to obtain your release,' he added.

'May the God of mercy give you his light and peace,' said Alleine sincerely. Turning away quickly to hide his emotion, Hugh limped off. He must ride speedily to Langport to break the sad news of Nicholas' death to Emma, but also to tell her of Robert's imminent release — both bitter and sweet together.

Hugh remained at Moorside for the next two weeks and attended Nicholas' funeral. A short service, conducted by Francis Bartlett, now elderly himself, was held at dead of night, for informers had even been known to report on such gatherings if more than five attended. Robert could hardly grieve over his father, for the sufferings Nicholas had endured since the loss of his wife Alice had set the old man's eyes ever more longingly on that land where treachery, pain and death can never enter and where he would be with the Saviour for ever.

But for Hugh it was far different. Riches, luxury and ambition had died for Hugh Wilmot at that moment when he was leaving the Palace of Whitehall. How ugly such abuse of love and plenty now seemed in Hugh's eyes! And the man whom he had admired deeply, one who had saved his life at such personal cost, was gone. With no family of his own and only his career as a capable barrister to fill the vacuum, Hugh felt totally bereft. If only he knew that light and peace of which Alleine had spoken! Perhaps one day he would ask Robert about these things, but for now he must return to his large and silent north London home without the merry prattle of little children, their quarrels and their tears, to distract his gloomy thoughts. Before he left Hugh thrust the king's letter into Robert's hand. 'In case you should ever need it again,' he said with a wry grin.

20.
An unforgettable night

'I keep wondering about our friends, Joan and Harry,' confessed Robert to Emma one day not long after Hugh had left. 'They were kind to me, and I fear for their safety. If the days are hard for us, what must it be like for those living in London?'

'Harry is not young,' Emma replied. 'Just suppose he is in prison and being cruelly treated. Didn't we hear about some in Aylesbury who were even under sentence of death for meeting as we do until our sovereign King Charles heard of it, and personally intervened?'

'You are always able to imagine the worst,' said Robert with a chuckle. 'But I must go and see if everything is well with them.' Leaving Thomas in charge of the printing press, Robert prepared once more for the long ride to London.

Thomas's attitude had softened towards his family since the loss of their baby daughter, but Nelly often shook her head wistfully and seemed diffident and troubled. Was the loss of her baby a punishment for her past sins, she asked herself. Would God ever forgive her?

The late August sun lit up the countryside as Robert rode away; already a tinge of autumn was touching the tops of the trees with gold. Much had happened since his last visit to London four years earlier when he had joyfully carried his bride back to Somerset. Three children had been born to them in quick succession: Alice, now a bright and talkative three-year-old; James, at eighteen months, kept his mother Emma in a constant state of alert; while little Philip, scarcely a month old, appeared to spend most of his time fast asleep at the moment.

During those years Robert's own mother, Alice, had died as a direct result of the persecution levelled mercilessly at any who wished to worship as Dissenters, independently of the state church. Now his father Nicholas, weakened by age and suffering, had also been taken. The Great Plague had swept though London the previous year, carrying a multitude of men, women and children to an unexpected and untimely grave, including Emma's father Bernard Allen and her brother Timothy. Pastor Joseph Alleine was still in prison...

Robert's thoughts ran on and on. His own two arrests and recent deliverance through the intervention of Hugh Wilmot gave him much cause for sober reflection and thankfulness to God, both for the privilege of suffering for his cause and for his mercy in setting him at liberty so speedily. What would the future hold? He hardly dared to think about it. Only the certain knowledge that the God in whom he trusted would never fail him gave him confidence to whistle a merry tune to himself as he jogged along.

It was a Sunday when Robert eventually arrived in the old City of London. Everywhere church bells rang out loudly, calling the people to worship. Robert wondered whether any Dissenting meetings were still open, but he imagined most would be worshipping in secret by now. He rode along Fleet Street, trying to avoid the potholes, and on up Ludgate Hill, past the once stern and splendid St Paul's Cathedral, its former graceful steeple now re-placed by a defiant square tower, challenging the crowded houses huddled below. Then, hurrying along Cheapside, along Poultry — all streets familiar to him from the days of his apprenticeship — he allowed himself a quick glance up Old Broad Street as he passed Threadneedle Street. That handsome board announcing 'The Sign of the Morning Star' now hung on one hinge, broken, dilapidated and desolate. He could even see the remains of the tragic red cross on the door, warning all around that death had visited that home. With a shudder Robert spurred his horse onwards, down Gracechurch Street and at last into Lombard Street, where Joan and Harry Lambert lived.

Unsure of his friends' exact location, Robert recalled that Sarah Allen had told him that the vast church of St Mary Woolnoth loomed high above the Lamberts' home. Several houses fitted such a description, but at his third attempt a grey-haired lady came to the door, peering out cautiously into the gathering dark. Suddenly her cheery face dimpled into smiles. 'Why, if it is not our good friend Robert Wilkes!' she exclaimed, throwing her arms around the tall and somewhat embarrassed visitor standing out-side. 'Now you bring your horse round the back, and I will have supper on the table in minutes,' she ordered, bustling off and calling out to Harry as she went.

That Sunday evening, 2 September 1666, spent with his friends was one that Robert would never forget. Harry too had been caught attending an illegal conventicle and fined heavily. On the first occasion he had paid the five pounds' fine, but it had cost all that he and Joan had been saving. Undeterred, the elderly couple had continued to attend the ministry of a Separatist preacher, and though they had taken the utmost caution not to be seen, some informer had gleefully reported them to the magistrate. This time Harry could not pay.

The prisons were already crowded beyond capacity with Quakers, Baptists and other Nonconformists, so instead of the ten pounds' fine, Harry and Joan's simple home had been raided by agents of the Justices of the Peace. With instructions to strip the place of goods to the value of ten pounds, ruthless men had confiscated tables, chairs, blankets, sheets, pots, pans, firewood, and even the meat Joan was about to cook. Everyone knew that the worth of these goods was far greater than ten pounds. 'But what could I do?' asked Harry, his voice breaking with emotion as he remembered that dreadful day. Through the generosity of neighbours and friends the Lamberts had been supplied with the basic essentials. But now they no longer dared to attend any more Nonconformist services. Apart from anything else, with their increasing years, they were unable to make the speedy escape that would be necessary to avoid capture if any of the secret locations where their meetings were held were discovered.

In turn Robert told Joan and Harry of his delightful three children, of the sad tragedy that had led to his mother's death and of the worthless barber-surgeon, Randy Cut-throat, who had betrayed them for providing

Joseph Alleine with a temporary shelter, and whose act had led to Nicholas' capture and subsequent death. These were indeed times of suffering for men and women of Christian conviction. As the evening wore on they sat talking, sharing memories of the past and encouraging each other to persevere. And still they talked until Harry's grey head gradually sank lower and lower onto his chest and a gentle snore suggested that they must all get to bed.

Exhausted from his long ride and the intense conversation of the evening, Robert fell into a deep sleep and was scarcely aware of the blustering wind that had risen and was rattling noisily around the small timber-framed house. But at about four in the morning, as the sky began to lighten, he was suddenly woken by the sound of several loud explosions, and a roaring louder than the roar of the wind. Then he heard screams and the rush of feet passing below along the footpath. Jumping from his bed, he dashed to the window and was horrified by what he saw. In the direction of the river the whole sky was lit up in lurid shades of red, orange and yellow. Fire!

The sight was terrifying. Not far away the tall spire of a church was ablaze like a fearsome beacon piercing the night sky. Roof timbers could be heard crashing to the ground. Then an even louder explosion seemed to rock the whole house. Now he could begin to feel the heat as the wind brought great columns of black smoke billowing across the city. Robert felt a fearful nausea creeping over him as he remembered the fire three years earlier that had destroyed the meeting house in the woods and taken his mother's life.

But one thought above all else gripped him. Somehow he must get Harry and Joan to safety. Who could tell whether the flames would reach this far? Certainly the

The Great Fire of London

wind was blowing in their direction. There was no time to spare. Without a moment's delay he rushed into the room where his friends were still sleeping, oblivious of the crisis. 'Fire! Fire!' he yelled, 'We must get out! Quick, get dressed, take anything you can carry… We must get out now!'

It took some moments before the elderly couple could grasp the situation. But at last, throwing on as many clothes as possible and, grabbing his old Bible along with one or two other books, Harry was ready, while Joan, still bleary with sleep, was almost too shocked to move quickly.

'Have you friends to whom we can go? asked Robert.

'Yes, yes,' Harry replied, 'in Southwark, across the London Bridge…'

'Then we must go now,' interrupted Robert. 'You and Joan will ride my horse and I will walk. Come, come, for I fear the bridge itself may catch alight.'

Now fully awake, Joan hastily gathered one or two valued items, wrapping them up in an old headscarf ready to carry — one that Robert had so often seen her wearing as she worked about the farm. Further explosions boomed nearby, followed by the ear-splitting sound of more falling timber. Joan began to sob in fear.

'I will say of the LORD, He is my refuge and my fortress: my God; in him will I trust,'[1] quoted Harry as they hurried down the stairs, for this was the very verse they had been speaking of the previous evening as they had shared together the pain and the mercies of recent years.

Out in the yard Robert's horse was whinnying in panic and it took him a few moments to calm it down enough to help Harry and Joan onto its back. By this time a black pall of smoke was filling the sky. Everywhere men and women were hurrying along, choking as they went, dragging

wailing children and carrying babies, all with one intent —
to reach the river.

Guided by Harry down numerous alleyways to avoid
the flames, Robert battled his way through the noise and
smoke, half dragging his unwilling horse along. Sometimes
the searing heat nearly overcame him. Would he ever get
through? He thought of Emma, of Alice, James and little
Philip. Perhaps the child would never know his father.
Then he reminded himself of the helpless couple relying on
him and urgently gasped his way forward, praying as he
went. At last he reached Lower Thames Street. The flames
were dangerously close now, their reflection in the dancing
water of the Thames making it look as if the river itself was
on fire. Crowds were pressing towards the Bridge, all with
the hope of reaching safety in Southwark. Others were
leaping into the barges tied along the quayside, throwing
their children down into the waiting arms of friends. Some
were even attempting to salvage their furniture.

Hurrying on towards the bridge, Robert saw to his
horror that the wind was blowing showers of burning
debris onto the first houses. It could only be a matter of
moments before they caught fire. Then curls of smoke
began rising into the air from the nearest house. Fiercely
beating out the sparks falling on his own clothes, Robert
rushed on. Only from halfway across the bridge did he look
back and see the houses behind him bursting into flames
one after another. How narrow their escape had been!

Along Southwark Street they hurried, and on into Thrale
Street where the Lamberts' friends, Samuel and Dorothy
Barnes, lived. By now the morning was well advanced, but
when Robert hammered on the door, no one answered for
some time, for, like everyone else, they were standing

Old London Bridge

transfixed at an upstairs window watching with horror as the scene of devastation unfolded across the river. At last, when Robert began shouting up at the window, they heard and quickly came down. With deep concern Dorothy begged the three to stay until it was safe to return to see whether Harry and Joan's home had survived the inferno. The unspoken question on everyone's mind was whether or not the fire would spread right across the bridge, and then set the Southwark houses ablaze.

Throughout that dreadful day they watched and waited as the flames ate up street after street north of the river. No one had time or thought to stop for refreshment until at last they saw with tremendous relief that a gap in the houses along the bridge had formed an effective firebreak and the flames were dying down. They were safe, at least for the time being.

For three long days the fire raged, consuming the houses and churches of London in its path. Interspersed with the roar of the fire was the sound of explosives, for the government had ordered the deliberate blowing up of houses before the advancing inferno to stop the flames leaping from house to house. Gone was the well-known skyline punctuated by steeples and spires. Even the mighty St Paul's Cathedral had been reduced to a blackened skeleton — nothing but devastation on all sides. 'I see little hope for our small home,' said Harry forlornly, shaken and unnerved by their terrible ordeal.

'When it is safe we will go and see,' answered Robert, but privately he knew that Harry was right. And he was. Early the following week, when the burning embers had cooled, Robert took Joan and Harry back across the bridge, past the pitiful remains of thousands of homes. Pots, pans and blackened timbers lay in their path as they picked their way across the wasteland which had once been the crowded streets of London.[2]

As they entered an area that was scarcely recognizable as Lombard Street, they gazed in shock and utter disbelief at the ruins of the city's proud financial houses that had once lined the street where the rich merchants of London had counted out their gold. All were gone. The only way to pinpoint the place where Harry and Joan's small home had once stood was to work out its approximate distance from the damaged remains of St Mary Woolnoth Church. Suddenly Joan gave a scream. She had spotted her own kettle — the very one that she had used on the evening before the fire — lying on its side in the gutter. Large tears rolled down Harry's honest old face — the first time he had shown any emotion. 'And what are we going to do now?' he asked at last.

'You are coming home with me,' replied Robert firmly. After returning to Southwark to thank their friends Samuel and Dorothy Barnes for their kindness and to request the loan of another horse, Harry and Joan set off for Somerset with Robert — back across London Bridge. With no possessions left in the world apart from the few items rescued before their flight, Robert could only remind them that nothing, neither fire nor persecution, could rob them of their eternal inheritance.

As they rode north, through street after street reduced to cinder and ash, the true scale of the disaster struck them dumb. All the familiar landmarks had disappeared. Only a rough sense of direction helped Robert guide his friends through the ruins. Where was the Royal Exchange? What about the grand old churches, solid for centuries, but now charred beyond recognition? The sad and deserted property in Old Broad Street had gone: the remains of the board that had once announced confidently 'The Sign of the Morning Star' now lay among the ashes. Robert bit his lip as he passed. How could he tell Emma, Sarah and Thomas about the loss? Even the forbidding walls of Newgate Prison had not been able to withstand the power of fire. How glad he was that Hugh Wilmot lived beyond to the north of the city, beyond the city wall — that defence from enemies in the past and now from the encroaching flames.

With immense relief the riders passed through New Gate and out into the open countryside. Joan, holding onto Harry as they jogged along, was still clutching her small bundle of possessions, wrapped up in her old scarf.

21.
THE AFTERMATH

Hugh Wilmot walked around the ruins of the London streets. Charred timbers and ash crunched under his feet. Hindered by his lame leg, he found it hard to clamber over the massive blackened beams lying haphazardly across his path — sad remnants of some elegant church where men and women had worshipped for generations. All around lay the burned remnants of homes reduced to rubble in a few devastating hours. Strewn everywhere he discovered little shoes, broken pottery, ruined furniture and dead animals. Rats scrambled over the debris at will. All was desolation. Hugh shook his head, sadly at first, then in dismay and disbelief. Why had this happened? Why? Yet he thought he knew. Surely God was angry with a land that persecuted men and women like Nicholas and Alice Wilkes, hounding them to an early grave. Surely two national disasters, first the Great Plague and now the Great Fire, within the space of a year were the response of heaven to such iniquity.

With his home now in Hampstead, a hilly area north of the city, away from the clatter and turmoil of London life, Hugh enjoyed views of open countryside. From that vantage point he could also gain a fine view of the city sprawling out below. On a clear day he could see as far as the River Thames, gleaming like a shiny snake in the distance. But on those fateful September days he, like many others, had watched in helpless astonishment as London was consumed in a blaze of destruction.

Sir Matthew Hale

Hugh had been swiftly promoted in the legal profession and had recently been appointed to serve as a barrister directly responsible to Sir Matthew Hale, Lord Chief Baron of the Exchequer. Hale, a kindly and merciful man, had been appointed by Parliament to oversee the vast numbers of legal claims arising from the loss of property in the fire. With a commission from Hale to investigate the extent of the devastation left by the fire, Hugh returned to Sir Matthew shocked and silent. The older man read his new assistant's thoughts. 'I fear God is angry with this land,' Hugh blurted out, almost before he could prevent himself.

'It is my fear also,' replied Sir Matthew unexpectedly. 'I have never forgotten a day — it must be five years ago now — when I presided over the Bedford Assizes. A young woman — I believe her name was Elizabeth Bunyan

— pleaded with me on behalf of her husband, John, a tinker, who had been imprisoned for preaching… She was only about twenty … his second wife … and was caring for his four young children, one of them blind — with nothing but charity to live on…'

'Yes,' encouraged Hugh. 'And could you help her?'

'I fear not, though if I had been more courageous I might have done so,' replied Sir Matthew sadly. 'I cannot forget that woman's last words, for she spoke boldly of a day when the "righteous Judge" should appear and vindicate such men as her husband, John. Perhaps that day has come.'

'I recently read a book by a man of that name,' confessed Hugh. 'Could it be the same, do you think, for he also was a tinker from Bedford and now suffers in prison for preaching?'

'Is that so?' responded Hale, his voice trembling. 'I pray you, show me the book, for I have heard many rumours of this man.'

'I will indeed, my lord,' Hugh answered, as he determined to read Mr Bunyan's words yet again for himself that very night.

After this Sir Matthew often spoke to Hugh of his concern for the Dissenters and their hearers, thousands of whom were suffering in prison. Seeing his sympathy, Hugh told him one day of a preacher he had met recently in Ilchester Jail, one by the name of Joseph Alleine. 'He is a good man, my lord,' said Hugh sincerely, 'and far from well. But nothing can stop him from preaching.'

'Are they all the same?' asked Sir Matthew in a despairing tone. 'Maybe I could urge His Majesty to show greater leniency for such.'

Perhaps out of fear, perhaps out of compassion, or perhaps even at the promptings of his Lord Chief Baron of the Exchequer, the king appeared anxious to ease restrictions on Nonconformists, and before long Joseph Alleine was released once more. Even the tinker-preacher, so it was rumoured, had been allowed out of Bedford Jail for the time being.

Before passing the tinker's book, *Grace Abounding to the Chief of Sinners*, to Sir Matthew, Hugh turned over its pages yet again. Two sentences struck him as he read: one concerned a day when the writer was wandering miserably up and down a field, feeling the weight of his sins, when he suddenly realized at long last that the mercy of God did not depend on his own moods, or even on his good deeds, but on the goodness of Christ that never changed; the other described the joy and freedom from the burden of guilt that the tinker felt at that moment:

> *As I was passing in the field, and that too with some dashes on my conscience ... suddenly this sentence fell upon my soul, Your righteousness is in heaven: I also saw, moreover, that it was not my good frame of heart that made my righteousness better, nor yet my bad frame that made my righteousness worse; for my righteousness was Jesus Christ himself, the same yesterday and today for ever... Now did my chains fall off my legs indeed, I was loosed from my afflictions... Oh! I thought, Christ! Christ! There was nothing but Christ ... before my eyes.*

'That must have been a good day for John Bunyan,' mused Hugh wistfully. Perhaps one day I too will be "loosed from my afflictions", and find what the tinker discovered.' He hardly realized that he too was edging ever nearer and nearer to that same understanding.

Meanwhile Harry and Joan Lambert found a kindly welcome awaiting them at Moorside. Never having had children of her own, Joan took great delight in helping Emma care for Alice, James and baby Philip. Harry, on the other hand, found it harder to settle. He tried to help Robert in the printing press, but it was a new skill for him and his large, work-roughened hands were ill-adapted to the delicate task of setting the tiny copper letters into the printing block.

Late one night, as Robert and Emma were discussing the problem, Emma suddenly had an idea: 'What about investing in poultry — chickens, ducks, geese and turkeys? We have much land that is lying fallow and our outhouses are never used. I am sure Harry would be expert at over-seeing such a project, and the sale of the eggs and meat would give him an income for himself and Joan.'

'Perhaps that would seem like a woman's work,' objected Robert.

'Ask him and see,' replied Emma sleepily.

Harry was delighted at the suggestion and accompanied Robert to market the following week to purchase stock. Before long little Alice came out each morning to help the old man gather the newly-laid eggs ready for sale.

With a farmer's eye, Harry could quickly recognize each bird, with its individual characteristics. But one day he was looking puzzled and troubled. 'Two of the hens are missing,' he told Robert.

'Perhaps a fox has been around,' suggested Robert.

But Harry shook his head doubtfully. 'I know only too well the evidence of a fox's activities,' he replied.

Three days later he discovered two handsome turkeys had gone. 'I fear a thief is at work,' he confided to Joan. But when two more birds had disappeared, Harry was sure. 'I will wait up each night until I catch the thief,' he declared robustly. And so he did. For two nights he sat in the corner of the shed, wrapped in blankets to keep warm. Nothing happened. On the third night he dozed off, but was suddenly awakened by a loud squawking. Fully alert now, he was just in time to see a figure making a quick escape, a sack in each hand. He thought it looked like a young man, but was too late to grab the thief.

After barricading the shed door more securely, Robert agreed to wait up with Harry two nights later. This time they hid in the bushes, where they could see clearly if anyone approached the shed. Unable to stay awake, Harry was soon snoring gently, but Robert was fully alert. Then he heard a creak in the undergrowth. He stiffened and watched. Very gradually a figure approached the shed door, carrying two empty sacks. Who was it? Just at that moment the moon emerged from behind a cloud and shone full on the thief's face. He instantly recognized the boy he had employed at the press and had been forced to dismiss. 'Sammy Coates!' yelled Robert, and sprang forward, grabbing the youth by the arm.

With a jerk Sammy tried to break free. Then he saw the tall, lumbering figure of Harry Lambert approaching, and felt the grip of his enormous hand on his shoulder. Sammy stood quite still, his face white with fear in the moonlight. He began to whimper like a whipped puppy. He knew full well that anyone caught stealing goods worth more than five shillings could be hung for the offence.

'And what do you think you are doing?' demanded Robert fiercely.

'We're starvin', me, my Mama and my little brothers; we're all starvin', ever since I lost my job with you...' His voice trailed off, and then continued, 'An' I know a man as can sell these birds for me, so I can buy some bread for them hungry little ones.' Robert gazed at the pale, tear-stained face in the moonlight. What was he going to do?

'Right,' he said at last. 'You go home, but I want you back here in the morning prompt. And if you are not here, you will be arrested for common theft ... and you know what that means.'

Sammy nodded dumbly, and was off in an instant, fearful lest Robert should change his mind.

Emma was wide awake by the time Robert crept into bed. Back and forth went the discussion as to the best course of action; at last Emma, whose quiet suggestions usually swayed her husband, said, 'Why not give him another chance in the press and reduce his money each week until he has paid for the birds he has stolen?'

When Sammy came next morning, clothed as neatly as he could, his face newly scrubbed, the fifteen-year-old was looking terrified. As Robert began with a stinging lecture on the sin of theft, the boy's eyes widened in panic, but when he concluded with Emma's suggestion, Sammy could only smile weakly through his tears. In fact Robert did need the extra help, for the business had been increasing steadily, and rumours of the favours shown him by none other than the King of England, together with the disgrace of the unpopular barber-surgeon, Randy Cutthroat, had grown in the telling. Added to this, Sammy had proved himself a good worker in the past, before Thomas arrived on the scene.

Emma took the opportunity to visit Sammy's mother, and was appalled at the condition of the home. Now and then she continued to call, taking with her small gifts of food, and even of bedding, for she soon saw that the family lacked many essentials. The gratitude Sammy's mother expressed for the kindness and the mercy shown to her son gave Emma the chance to speak to the needy woman of a Saviour who forgives sins and who has mercy on the broken and destitute.

Since Hugh's intervention with the king on Robert's behalf, no magistrate or informer had dared to molest the Langport Meeting as it gathered each week, usually at Moorside. Thomas and Nelly were attending regularly, and Nelly, now expecting another child, seemed assured at last of God's acceptance and forgiveness. And on some occasions a poorly-clad woman could be seen sitting at the back, and listening intently to the words of Francis Bartlett, or those of Harry Lambert, or even of Robert himself, who sometimes preached instead of their ageing pastor.

22.
LOST AND FOUND

'I fear Pastor Joseph is dying,' Robert confided sadly to Emma one day in 1668. 'As I was delivering proofs in Taunton I met Master John Mallack, whom he has often stayed with, and he gave me news of him.'

'I thought his health was failing when he and Theodosia were with us,' responded Emma. 'How wicked of our government to treat good men like him in the way it has! And he is only young — not yet thirty-five. That fearful prison…!' Her voice trailed off as she thought how easily Robert too could have been broken by such circumstances if Hugh Wilmot had not interceded with the king for him.

'I hear he is going soon to Bath to take the waters,' Robert replied. 'It is his only hope, it seems. I must visit him before he goes.'

But the day before he had hoped to go, Robert was surprised by a visit from his friend Hugh Wilmot. Hugh had become a regular visitor to Moorside since the Great Fire. His work, listening day after day to claims for legal compensation from men who had lost everything in the tragedy that had enveloped the city, was harrowing and exhausting. Sir Matthew Hale often delegated some of the less complicated cases to Hugh, but even these caused the younger man distress. Some claims were possibly fraudulent, and therefore needed investigating. Day after day Hugh found himself poring over legal documents relating to the different cases until his eyes ached. So when he felt in need of a few days' rest, just one place drew him back time and again: Moorside Farm.

The summer months of 1668 had been sultry and dry. With London being steadily rebuilt and the lives of its citizens gradually returning to a degree of normality, Hugh decided to pay his friends in Somerset another visit. After a long and exhausting ride, he at last reached the crossroads leading to Taunton in one direction and Somerton in the other. Just before he headed down the winding lane to the farm he stopped to rest for a few moments. How good to surprise Robert and Emma with a visit! And then there was that elderly couple, Joan and Harry Lambert — Hugh had been delighted to hear of their happiness in their new home. He smiled to himself as he thought of the family. Little Alice, undoubtedly his favourite, was now five; her quaint ways fascinated him, and somehow a strange bond had grown up between them. Her younger brother, now known as Jamie, was almost four and as restless and full of mischief as Alice was serious. Two-year-old Philip, meanwhile, surveyed the world around him with large solemn eyes, and appeared to be silently weighing up the strengths and weaknesses of everyone he met.

At that moment, as Hugh halted in the lane leading to Moorside, he heard the sound of a cart rumbling along in the direction of Taunton. At any moment it would cross his path, so he decided to wait until it had gone.

'Good day,' he called out cheerily, as the wagon driver passed him, lashing his horse mercilessly at the same moment. No reply. The man looked shifty, surly, and Hugh grew suspicious. He glanced at the goods lying open on the back of the cart. What a strange assortment — a kettle, firewood, a small bed, a broken table, even a pile of wooden plates and a toy or two!

Then Hugh guessed the man's dastardly business. 'Stop, in the name of the king!' he yelled, blocking the wagon's onward path with his horse.

'And who, may I ask, are you?' demanded the driver angrily.

'Hugh Wilmot, barrister to Sir Matthew Hale, Chief Baron of the Exchequer, for His Majesty, Charles, King of England,' replied Hugh grandly. 'I demand to know your business.'

The wagon driver paled visibly. The name 'Wilmot' still had the power to instil fear into the heart of every West Country man as he recalled the exploits of Lord Henry Wilmot both during the fearful Civil War and afterwards.

'These are goods confiscated from a woman found attending an illegal conventicle at Moorside. I take them to Taunton market for sale to raise the dues, for she cannot pay the fine,' replied the driver. Looking scared now, for it was clear that the worth of the goods he was carrying was far in excess of any fine due, he added in a whining tone, 'Let me pass now, I pray you, good sir.'

'By no means,' was the stern reply. 'What is the woman's name, and where does she live?'

'Madam Coates, from Pibsbury,' replied the driver reluctantly. In a flash Hugh recollected his friend Robert's story about the young man, Sammy Coates, caught stealing poultry, and of his poverty-stricken family.

'In the name of the king, I demand that you return those goods immediately. I will follow you to that woman's house,' he roared in an authoritative voice. With no option but to obey, the wagon driver turned his animal around in the road and slowly rumbled back to Pibsbury, followed all the way by Hugh Wilmot.

When Ellen Coates, sitting sobbing in her cottage doorway surrounded by her bewildered children, saw the wagon approaching, she thought they had returned to take yet more away. Her relief and her gratitude to Hugh were pitiful and intense, and before he left the scene, he gave the frightened woman a note written in the name of Sir Matthew Hale, stipulating that she was to be left alone in future. Whether or not he had any authority to do so, he did not stop to enquire.

With a degree of amusement Robert and Emma listened to Hugh's tale. True, certain men claiming to be sent by the local magistrates had burst into the meeting three days earlier, but when Robert had displayed his highly valued letter, signed by the king himself, they hastily withdrew. Robert suspected immediately that these men were only common thieves, for the Taunton magistrates knew better than to molest the gatherings at Moorside. They must have spotted poor Ellen Coates sitting at the back, and found in this defenceless woman an easy target for their activities.

The children greeted Mr Hugh with delight, Alice clinging to his hand, while Jamie danced in circles around him.

'I'm sorry to tell you,' said Robert, after the excitement had calmed and Hugh was refreshed, 'that our good friend Pastor Alleine is seriously ill. I hear he has lost the use of his limbs and sinks fast. I plan to visit him in his Taunton home tomorrow. It may indeed be my last chance to see him, for he plans to travel to Bath to take the waters; it is his last hope.' When Hugh asked if he might accompany him, Robert readily agreed.

The sight of the pathetically weakened preacher lying on a couch, unable even to lift one finger to help himself, was grievous. While Robert could hardly restrain his tears, Hugh felt a surge of anger against a state that allowed a tall, strong man not yet in his mid-thirties to be so desperately reduced by the cruelty inflicted upon him in Ilchester Jail.

Joseph Alleine quickly read the faces of the two men, and spoke seriously to both. 'Farewell, farewell, my dear friends,' he said in a low voice. And then, looking straight at Robert, he continued, 'I beseech you, if I never see your face again, that you go home and live what I have preached to you.' Addressing Hugh he added, 'Oh, let not my wasted strength, my useless limbs, rise up in judgement against you at the great day of the Lord. Turn, turn while yet there is time.' And to both of them he whispered slowly and deliberately, 'Oh, live on God! For the Lord's sake go home, but beware of worldly comforts and worldly cares...' As his voice grew weaker, Theodosia, who seldom left his side, signalled that he could take no more.

Robert and Hugh rode the twelve miles back to Moor-side in silence, each buried in his own thoughts. Robert could see that Hugh, a deeply sensitive man, had been profoundly affected by the dying preacher's words.

As they arrived back, they discovered that a crisis had arisen at Moorside: little Alice was missing. Emma thought she might have gone in search of her father or of Mr Hugh, to whom she was devoted. Emma, together with Joan and Harry, had searched everywhere they could, through barns, outhouses, among the woods that surrounded the farm, even down the rhyne, but there was neither sight nor sound of the child. 'Perhaps she has tried to go to Pibsbury to see Grandma Sarah or even Nelly,' suggested Emma.

Robert immediately set off for Pibsbury, while Hugh began to scan the further woods and fields. But both men returned, reporting no sign of the five-year-old. As darkness was beginning to gather their anxiety increased. Then a fearful thought struck Hugh. Could she possibly have wandered as far as the River Parrett? Perhaps she wanted to explore the old ruined house where the Langport Meeting had often gathered for worship? Without sharing his fears, Hugh determined to go and look, while Robert checked again all around the farm before trying to comfort Emma.

Eerie and ghostly in the moonlight, the deserted house stood hidden in dense undergrowth. Only the cry of the occasional owl broke the silence. Carefully Hugh examined room after room, casting the beam of his flickering lamp into every darkened corner. Alice was certainly not there. He was wrong. Puzzled and anxious, he left the house and stood on the riverbank, the cheerful gurgle of water rushing over boulders drowning every other sound. Then suddenly Hugh gave a suppressed scream. There, caught

River scene

on the root of an old tree, hung a little white sock — it must be Alice's!

Frantically Hugh began to search along the bank, calling Alice's name as loudly as he could. He poked a stick he had found into every clump of bushes. Then he saw a small red shoe. A chill of dreadful fear brought the sweat pouring down Hugh's face. Either the child had fallen in the river and had been swept far away by now, or ... maybe, just maybe ... she was nearby...

Was that an answering cry? Hugh stood quite still, listening intently. Yes, he was sure of it — there was a child crying somewhere out there in the dark. Stumbling on, his lame leg making progress more difficult, Hugh stopped, called, listened and called again. Then he saw her; curled up on the bank, her small face tear-stained in the moonlight.

'I'm lost, Mr Hugh,' said the child, as if it was the most normal thing in the world for him to find her like that. 'I came to explore the old house; then I got lost, but I knew you would come.' Alice was barefooted, for both her shoes and her socks had come off as she scrambled along the riverbank trying to find her way out of the bushes. She was shivering in her thin cotton dress.

Gently Hugh picked the little girl up and battled his way back through the undergrowth to where he had left his horse. As he went he silently lifted up a prayer to God — the God he had so long rejected — a voiceless prayer of gratitude.

With tears of relief the family greeted Hugh as he carried Alice through the low farm door, and seated her, chilled but unharmed, on a kitchen chair. When all the fuss had died down and Alice had been suitably rebuked before being safely tucked up in bed, Hugh told his side of the story.

'Mr Hugh,' said Alice the next day, 'would you read me a story, one from Grandpa's old book that he was always reading?' Confidently the child placed Nicholas' tattered Bible on Hugh's lap and climbed up expectantly herself.

'What story would you like, Alice?' asked Hugh, scarcely knowing where to turn.

'Grandpa used to look after sheep, and so did my pa a long time ago. Can I have the one about the sheep that got lost?'

Overhearing her daughter's request, and knowing that Hugh would not be able to find the right place in the Bible, Emma quickly flicked over the pages until she came to

Luke 15 and handed the book back to Hugh. Carefully Hugh read the parable of the lost sheep and of the shepherd who left the ninety-nine that were already safe and went out looking for his lost one.

'I was lost like that,' said Alice thoughtfully, 'but you found me. Have you ever been lost, Mr Hugh?'

'Yes, yes,' said Hugh suddenly. 'Twice, little Alice, twice. Once your grandpa found me when I was badly hurt in a battle. That's when I got this nasty scar on my face. And once...' He hesitated and then said, 'Maybe I have been lost like that sheep in the story, and perhaps the Shepherd has found me, but I'm not quite sure yet.'

In reply Alice, who understood little of Hugh's meaning, put up her hand and stroked Hugh's face. 'I love that old scar,' she said.

At last the sword — the cruel sword of both war and state that had devoured and destroyed Dissenter and Royalist alike in seventeenth-century England — had been broken by the power of God in the lives of two far different men, Robert Wilkes and Hugh Wilmot.

Postscript:
The days that followed

Although the Moorside Farm epic told in this book ends in 1668, the persecution against the Dissenters was far from over. For the next twenty years it continued, sometimes with vicious and fearful intensity, until the 'Glorious Revolution' of 1688 when James II was forced into exile and William of Orange and Mary came to the throne in his place. The Toleration Act was finally passed in May 1689, freeing the Dissenting churches from the burden of constant harassment.

The temporary easing of persecution for Dissenting, or non-episcopal, churches in 1668, following the Great Fire, did not last for long, for on 11 April 1670 a Second Conventicle Act was passed by Parliament. The sufferings of the Quakers and Nonconformist groups, such as the Baptists and the Independents, also known as Congregationalists, then became more brutal than ever. Certain areas of the country fared better than others, depending on the mood of the local authorities, but in some parts it continued unabated. In Bedfordshire, where John Bunyan was imprisoned, circumstances were harsh. Informers could now receive a handsome percentage of the fines levied on those caught attending a conventicle as a reward for their dastardly work. This encouraged many a man, down on his luck, to try his hand at spying on his neighbours and former friends. Even children were encouraged to report sightings of townsfolk — traders, merchants and farmers — who might be meeting in secret for religious purposes, and to discover where they gathered to worship.

A document has survived detailing the fines and confiscation of goods suffered by believers in Bedford. Many had their tools of trade seized; even the food on the table was sequestrated, leaving their children hungry. The account ends with these words: 'Poor and industrious families are utterly ruined, some made wholly incapable to provide for their future subsistence.'

Somerset was another region badly affected. Although in this narrative Robert and the Langport Meeting were freed from persecution by the intervention of Hugh Wilmot, this was not generally true. *The Axminster Ecclesiastica*, recently reissued under the title *After the Puritans* by the Mayflower Christian Bookshop, Southampton, details the sufferings of a church in the same area in which this story is set. Nearby Loughwood Meeting, not far from Axminster,[1] hidden away in the forest, also suffered constant harassment, as did the Newhouse Meeting, high up in the Blackdown Hills. In Bristol worshippers were driven out onto the streets, beaten with swords and pikestaffs, their buildings torched before their eyes.

One man, a Job Spurgeon, possibly one of C. H. Spurgeon's ancestors, records his sufferings in Chelmsford

Jail, where for fifteen weeks he had nothing to lie on but straw and had no protection from the extreme cold until he became so weak that he could not even lie down if he had wanted to.

In some respects a number of the Dissenters increased their own sufferings by allowing themselves to become involved politically in a vain attempt to change the succession to the throne. The Roman Catholic brother of Charles II, James, was heir apparent as Charles had no legitimate children, despite having twelve illegitimate ones. With such a man as James on the throne, the Dissenters could only foresee a fearsome increase of their sufferings. After the fall of the Cavalier Parliament, that engineer of legislation such as the Conventicle Act and the Five Mile Act, intended to crush Puritanism and Dissent, a new government — the Whigs — came to power in 1679. Many Dissenters supported the new Whig government, hoping for political answers to the constant abuse they suffered. But when the Whigs tried three times to introduce an Exclusion Bill to stop James from succeeding to the throne, Charles II was furious and the Whigs fell from power in 1681. Looking for a scapegoat on whom to vent his anger, Charles and his Royalist supporters picked on the Dissenters, and their sufferings increased dramatically.

Then in 1683 came yet another attempt to rid the country of Catholic James — the Rye House Plot. Hatched by former Cromwellian soldiers, it purposed to murder both Charles and his brother James on their way back from the Newmarket Races and put the nominally Protestant James Duke of Monmouth on the throne instead. This plot miscarried badly, and Monmouth fled to Holland. As the plot had been supported by many Dissenters, its failure led to a still greater intensification of persecution for their churches. G. R. Cragg, in his work entitled *The Great Persecution*, describes the situation:

> *Fines of staggering magnitude were levied on the more prosperous Nonconformists. Their homes were pillaged, their goods seized. Even the humblest members found no immunity. Those who owned little lost it all. Tradesmen were ruined. In some districts the dislocation of business was serious, and the cry was raised that the economic prosperity of the country was threatened. In the streets the Nonconformists were exposed to such violent abuse that their leaders hesitated to venture abroad.*[2]

The great Dr John Owen was also imprisoned for a time, along with other prominent Dissenters, accused of being implicated in the plot. Such suspicions were unfounded, but when James did eventually become king in 1685, he, together with his Lord Chief Justice George Jeffreys, determined to punish the Nonconformists and to wreak as much damage on their churches as possible. The elderly Richard Baxter was arrested and brought to trial by the merciless Judge Jeffreys, who would gladly have had the old man whipped from one side of London to the other, but was overruled by more merciful men.

But worst of all was the Monmouth Rebellion, which Robert in the narrative would have lived to see and in which many young men of the same age as his son Jamie were involved. In one last desperate attempt to rid the country of Roman Catholic James II, hundreds of Dissenters joined in the plan to bring the Duke of Monmouth back to English shores and, together with a Scottish army, to march on London, oust James II from the throne and set up the duke in his place. A catastrophic failure, the Battle of Sedgemoor, fought less than ten miles north of Langport, was strongly supported by West Country Dissenters with an unfounded confidence in the integrity of the handsome Duke of Monmouth and a final hope of bringing their sufferings to an end. Officiating at the Bloody Assizes, Judge George Jeffreys, assisted by other judges, sentenced hundreds of men to death by hanging, others to be hung, drawn and quartered — the ultimate punishment for treason. Body parts were displayed around the countryside as an object lesson for any future rebels. More than 800 men were transported to Barbados to be sold into slavery, many of whom perished on the voyage.

Fine and godly men were executed at this time, including the two grandsons of the Particular Baptist leader, William Kiffin. One of these, also called William and only nineteen years of age, said on the night before he was hung, 'Oh, how great were the sufferings of Christ for me, beyond all I can undergo! How great is the glory to which I am going! It will soon swallow up all our sufferings here.'

But James II's own time was short. His nobles and barons gradually became disillusioned with his bad judgements and biased decisions. Then when his second wife, Mary of Modena, unexpectedly gave birth to a son, a Catholic heir,[3] after fifteen years of marriage, there was widespread dismay and a determination to invite James's eldest daughter by his first marriage, Mary, and her husband William of Orange to take the crown of England. James fled in panic; William and Mary were proclaimed as king and queen on 13 February 1689.

The Act of Toleration followed later that year, at last giving freedom to worship according to the dictates of their own consciences to all except Roman Catholics and Quakers, provided that they took oaths of allegiance to the Crown. Nonconformists and Dissenters might now build their own places of worship, appoint their own preachers and worship without using the *Book of Common Prayer*, not fearing that their meetings would be disrupted at any moment and they themselves subjected to prison or hefty fines.

Although they would still be deprived for many years to come of a number of privileges granted to their fellow citizens, the Dissenters of the seventeenth century had endured through days of fearsome persecution. Their courage and insistence upon spiritual and scriptural principles had proved stronger than the sword of civil government that had tried to vanquish their churches. To them, and to many like them who suffer in our own day, a time will come when they will receive the accolades of heaven and hear such words as:

Blessed is the man who remains steadfast under trial, for when he has stood the test he will receive the crown of life, which God has promised to those who love him (James 1:12, ESV).

Notes

Chapter 2 — At what cost?
1. A pound (£1) was worth twenty shillings.

Chapter 3 — How can I forgive?
1. Luke 23:33-34.
2. A sovereign was a gold coin worth £1.

Chapter 4 — The past explained
1. Deuteronomy 29:29.
2. Psalm 37:4.

Chapter 8 — The call of home
1. Proverbs 18:14.

Chapter 9 — To print ... or not to print?
1. Psalm 130:7.

Chapter 14 — The two Alices
1. 2 Tim. 3.12

Chapter 15 — The Conventicle Act

1. Not all magistrates enforced the Conventicle Act with equal rigour, but in the West Country, where this story is set, it was followed with brutality.
2. John 16:33.
3. See Psalm 62:8.
4. John 14:27.

Chapter 20 — An unforgettable night

1. Psalm 91:2.
2. Four-fifths of old London were destroyed, including 13,200 houses, eighty-seven churches, six chapels and other important buildings such as the Guildhall. Over 200,000 lost their homes.

Postscript — The days that followed

1. See picture on page 106.
2. G. R. Cragg, *The Great Persecution*, Cambridge University Press, 1957, p.26.
3. The suspicion was abroad, due to the 'timeliness' of his birth, that this baby, called by some the 'warming-pan baby', was smuggled into the royal apartments in a warming-pan, and was not in fact the child of James and Mary of Modena.

In this exciting novel Faith Cook gives rich spiritual insights from suffering and persecuted Christians in the age of John Bunyan. A gripping read for everyone young and old. Sadly very relevant to much of our modern world.

John Grier
Evangelical Bookshop, Belfast

Sales of this book help to promote the missionary work of EP in making good Christian literature available at affordable prices in poorer countries of the world and training pastors and preachers to teach God's Word to others.